SHADOWS OF AZATHOTH

Horrific Tales of Vampiric Darkness

MICHAEL W. FORD

SHADOWS OF AZATHOTH
HORRIFIC TALES OF VAMPIRIC DARKNESS

By MICHAEL W. FORD

Copyright © 2009-2011 by Michael W. Ford
Edited by Tom Tabori
Cover Design: Chaos-Temple © by KristianWahlin, used with kind permission.
'Dead body' by Karl N.E.
Vampire and Nosferatu Art by Nestor Avalos
ISBN-13: 978-1466470194
ISBN-10: 1466470194

All rights reserved. No part of this book, in part or in whole, may be reproduced, transmitted, or utilized, in any form or by any means electronic or mechanical, including photocopying, recording, or by any information storage and retrieval system, without written permission in writing from the publisher, except for brief quotations in critical articles, books and reviews.

Information:
Succubus Productions
PO Box 926344
Houston, TX 77292
USA
Website: http://www.luciferianwitchcraft.com
email: succubusproductions@yahoo.com

SHADOWS OF AZATHOTH

Horrific Tales of Vampiric Darkness

MICHAEL W. FORD

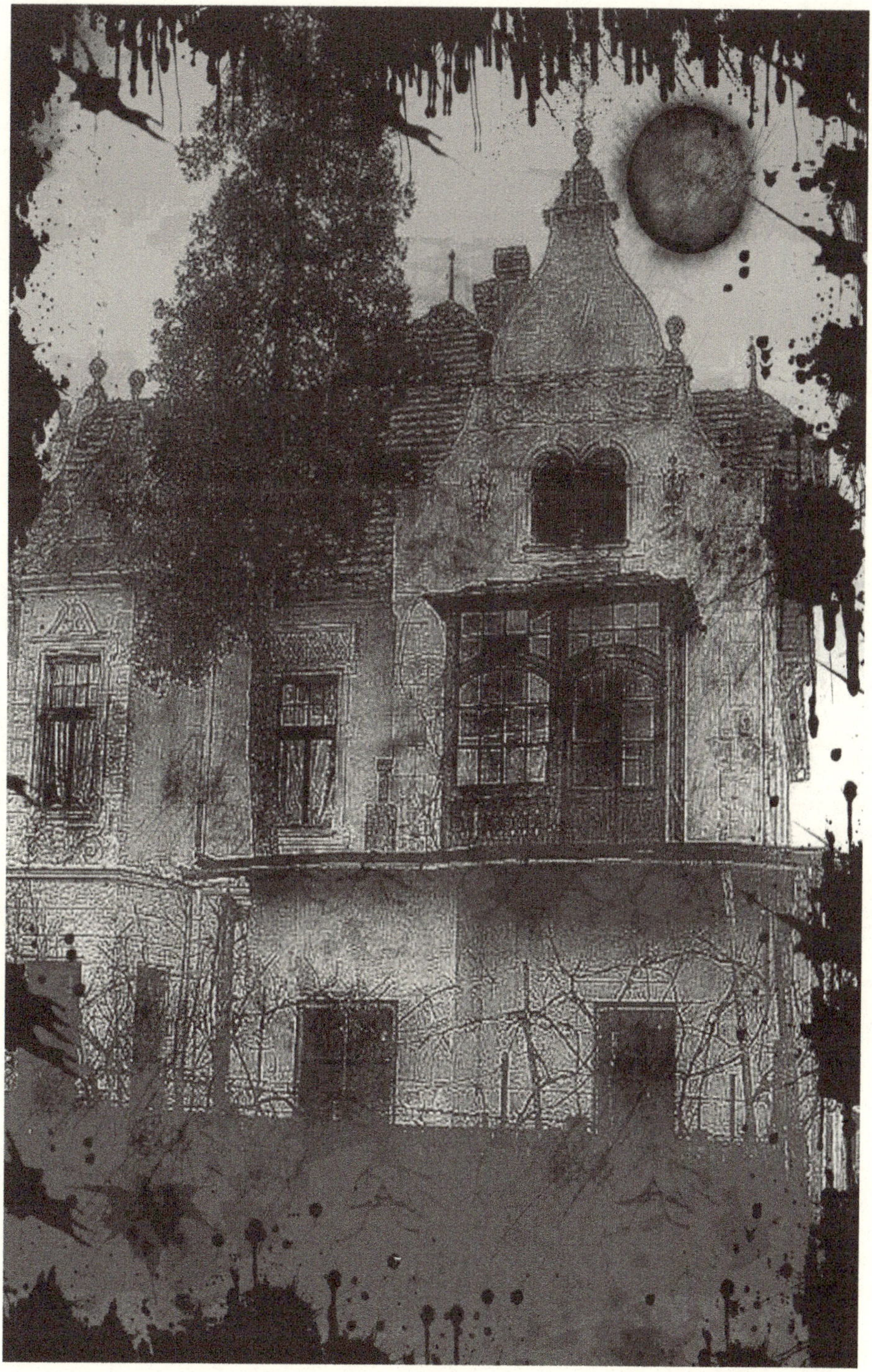

Magick and opening gateways in the mind is always conducted by the imagination.

What if this could be done unknowingly?

What if it was always meant that way?

Perhaps it is just a story.

Perhaps it is more…

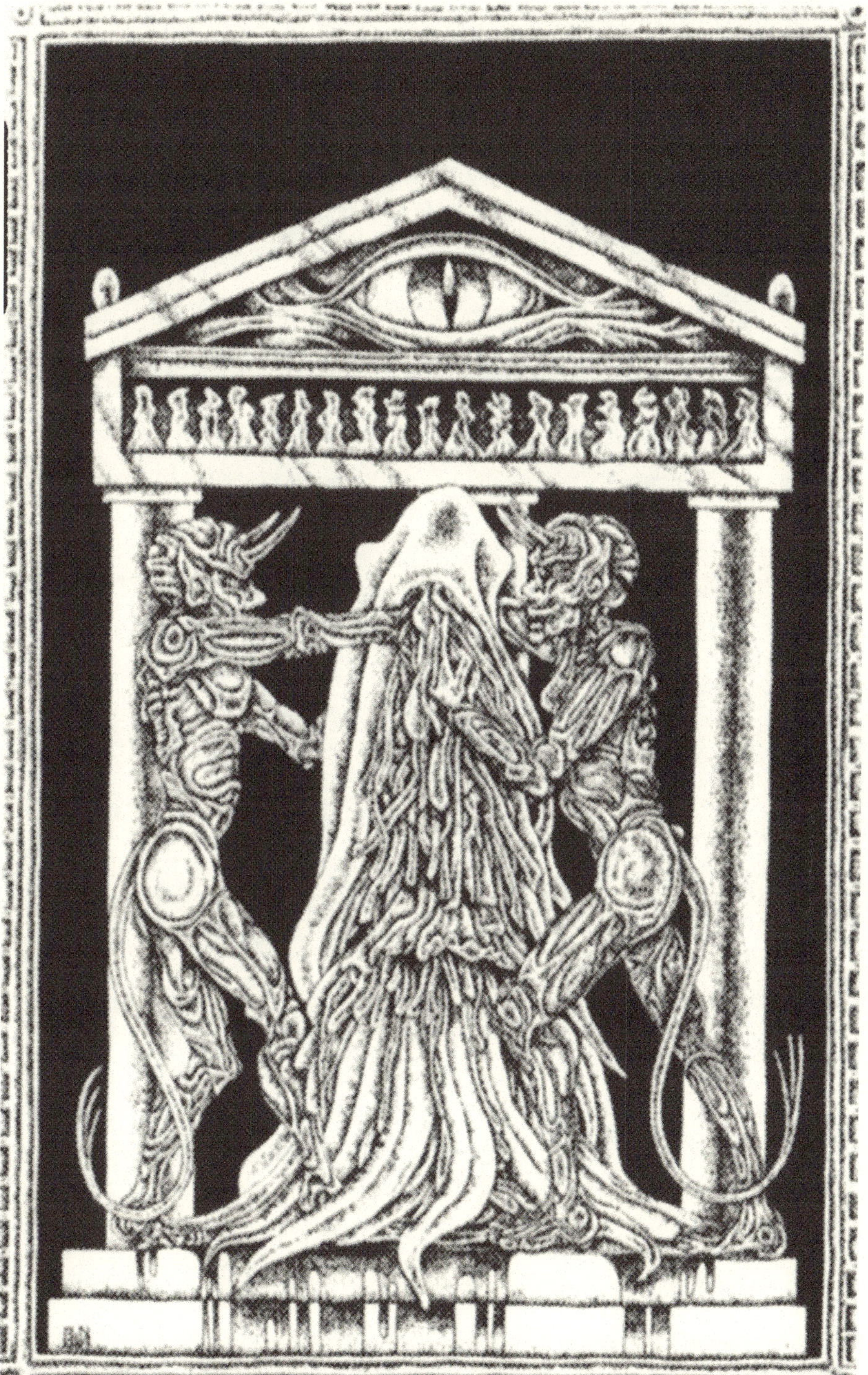

CONTENTS

Shadows of Azathoth…pg 13

The Hungering One…pg 85

Cult of the War God - *The Hidden Vampiric Cult of Tiamat*… *pg 95*

SHADOWS OF AZATHOTH

BY MICHAEL W. FORD

PREFACE

AZATHOTH, whose origins are nameless, who beholds his being as timeless and haunting into our living world. With each tick of a clock, each alarm which rings, time passes judgment on flesh. It withers, growing loose, white, and sick. Regard it as the natural passage, the very kiss of a God who many perceive as love. Nature hates us all, yet we try still to take care of her.

Azathoth is known by a select and secretive few as the sorcerer whose blood wants to multiply here in this world. It wants to bleed forth into mouths, black and stench-ridden. Like the desperate cry of a parent who has lost their child in a shopping mall. Azathoth is perceived as an ancient daemon sitting upon the Throne of Chaos, growing stronger with each soul devoured. The children of Azathoth feed him, that great shadow who exists where heat is less, where water is only a blinding abyss and where air breathes the wings of insects and crop killers. Life is precious and Azathoth knows this more than any. Azathoth not only exists to manifest alone in the world, yet to usher forth the elder ones – among them the Seven Daemons of Babylonia – a chaotic devouring and fierce spiritual force which takes the shapes and parts of insects, wolves, rabid dogs, dragons or large serpents and more.

His dwelling is a great tower, a mixture of rusted metal and stone, aged, yet timeless in design. At the top of the tower, multitudes of bats and crows intermix and fly about, screeching – Azathoth hears all. His sorceries are powerful; timeless… he is the Lord of Darkness, chaos and screaming, black eyed children who drink blood to honor him. He is shadow and this world imprisons him. For every soul given to the

Qlippothic forms which brought him here, enthroned him as a type of father to keep them in strength.

Skies, overcast crimson which occasional lightning touch all around. Trees, no longer producing the oxygen they should, twist and curl into spider-like tendrils which echo the spirit of the Vampiric form of Azathoth. The Tower above is the center of terror – night black blood dancing slowly in serpent fashion down walls of hands clawing to get out, all crying forth to the Throne, encircled in fire and darkness. Shadows serve him, his blindness is only a myth, he can see and he can hunt.

PART ONE

Brandon Kestle has held an interest in the Magick arts for many years. Not particularly looking the part, his balding stature is hardly a consideration for someone practicing forbidden arts. In a world of internet, he found theories of Azathoth, this site and this place which houses secrets – search them out he thought. His career as a web designer no doubt grants him the time to travel, on vacations to visit remote locations where they are whispered to gather. He did just that. Brandon's interest in Magick is as serious as any – study this and practice that, he learned to control the mind.

Magick is differentiated from Magic wherein individuals perform stage tricks. Magick is considered as old as humanity itself. Magick in the Western tradition is creative in nature; it involves visualization and imagination. The process of ritual is to align oneself with a higher consciousness, to cause self-evolution. Since the time of the Ancient Egyptians, Magick has been a means of self-transformation and acquiring knowledge. With the modern age of various types of Magick, often there is still the inherent aim of creativity and wisdom, yet the darker paths of Magick also remain. As equally a part of our collective psyche, Abyssic Magick is the calling forth of the primal and daemonic, wherein our dark consciousness is illuminated and brought in union with the higher aspects of our consciousness.

We find as such the workings of the primal cults of Azathoth and Cthulhu, those which bring power and transform the practitioner either into prey of the dark ones, or to be indwelt by primal powers which in turn transform our consciousness into Gods and Goddesses, with predatory instincts fully in place.

In a bookstore in Bucharest he met a clerk, who in broken English spoke of a cult of Magick, after noticing Brandon leafing through some of the darker titles of the place. After a conversation expressing interest, the clerk, a short, wide eyed middle aged type that seemed eager to suggest – from bad titles he knew were garbage or the type you could download anywhere from a bit torrent site –but this "Cult of Azathoth" seemed at least curious…Brandon wanted to see some local sites and was planning the obligatory "Dracula" scenic tour to some sites where the legendary hero fought off invaders.

Knowing that some representatives of the "Cult of Azathoth" meet at the Dante Café, a small, cramped coffee bar where one could sit comfortably considering the size of the building and discuss nearly anything, either over coffee or the liquor of your choice. Finding his way to Kogalniceanu Street two nights from this meeting with the clerk in the bookstore, a fine Thursday evening, clear and only a bit chilly – September is always a beautiful time nearly anywhere, he strode in the bar in a gray fleece coat – a little much for the evening but it was all he had brought to Europe, he knew not to pack a lot and avoid looking too much like a tourist – something he learned by living in New York City.

Looking around the light cloud of smoke in the room, he could make out a dozen or so faces talking, laughing and drinking. It was obvious who the members of the group were based on how they were situated in the room – in a corner with a seeming huddle, talking. Small chairs were manipulated around to where the six individuals were sitting. The one speaking, a middle aged man, white hair with specks of gray and black was dressed casual in a white button down shirt with a brown jacket over it, dark eyes and unshaven for about two days, a dark moustache really set his face out. Looking up in an inquisitive manner, he noticed Brandon standing near the bar. Looking down and paying attention to the group once again, Brandon thought he should approach them soon, or else he was wasting his time.

Sipping on an espresso, Brandon planted himself at the edge of the bar, when he noticed the man stood up from his seat and walked over to the bar. Ordering a glass of red wine, he looked over and said "hello!" to Brandon.

"I was only staring because I was told a coven met here; I have had an interest in Magick for a long time now." Brandon chirped nervously.

"What makes you think we would talk to you, who told you this?" the man said dryly.

Brandon's eyebrows rose slightly, "A bookstore led me here; I travel on business as a web designer so I thought to visit Bucharest."

"Is it so…you still did not answer, why should we care?" the man's eyes were intense.

"I'm sorry, I'm afraid I am not great at introductions. My name is Brandon Kestle, I live in New York City, USA. I have had an interest in the dark aspects of Magick for many years." Brandon chirped up facing the man directly.

"Good to meet you, I am Nicolae. I am an owner of a tourist agency here." the man said with a warm smile. "We have lived in this area for many years, our family has been involved in Magick for a very long time" Nicolae continued.

The group was now looking curiously at Brandon…he notices and senses a small amount of anxiety beneath the surface.

"I have studied Magick for some time, my main interests are Enochian, Crowley." Brandon spoke in a louder voice; the café had quite a few people now that it was past dark.

"Ah, yes. Aleister Crowley…well we have a mythological interest, yes in Magick from a bit older than he…Crowley, no offense if you are a Thelemite." Nicolae said watching his pronunciation.

Thelemite, Brandon thought, the ones who work through Aleister Crowley's system of Magick, not specifically anything "satanic" related or whatnot. Magick and Crowley's view of it was self-transformation, expanding consciousness and nothing at all like it was portrayed in the media.

"I am very interested indeed" Brandon smiled carefully, "I am not a part of any group or order, haven't found the right one yet. I have joined a few lodges here and there but no long term workings." his smile nearly fading with a sense of awkwardness.

"You may wish to meet the group, would you care to join us…?" Nicolae grinned and with his right hand guided Brandon's arm.

Feeling the anxiety growing a bit, sweat formed on Brandon's brow as Nicolae walked him over to the others…none smiling.

"I would like to introduce you to my friends and fellow seekers, everyone, this is Brandon…what did you say your last name was", it was almost as if Nicolae was merely faking the forgetfulness of not remembering his last name.

"Brandon Kestle, I am on vacation from the USA, New York City." Brandon said in a loud enough voice to be heard by the six. He did not want to mention the Dracula tour in fear of them laughing at him.

"Good to meet you Mr. K-est-el", carefully sounding his name, "I am Ramon" said a shorter man, smiling and offering his hand.

The second and third were obviously a couple, older, around 45 or so, the woman had gray streaks through her hair…sharp Romanian features and dressed in a gray and black suit with a knee high skirt and sharp black shoes. The man, wearing a gray blazer extended his hand, thin glasses with a moustache. Sitting next to them is a young girl, who must be their daughter or someone closely related. She appears to be about 9 or so. Brandon notices her posture is straight and at first glance appears to be well behaved, yet not so interested in what is going on around her.

"Hello, I am Anton and this is Erzsebet." the Romanian accent strong, but the English distinct.

"Nice to meet you" Brandon said respectfully while shaking hands with both of them.

"We don't bathe in blood, I promise" Erzsebet playfully interjects. The tense feeling is lifting and Brandon's shoulders fall a bit in relief that they at least have a sense of humor.

They don't offer to introduce the girl, who just sits there reading a book.

Nicolae lowered his right arm, extending to the other two standing.

"Brandon, this is Stephan and this is Tomas"…Nicolae stated with a soft smile.

"Good to meet you both." Brandon said, making sure to make eye contact with both.

"Please Mr. Kestle, pull up a chair." Tomas moved the chair over enough to allow Brandon's chair to be moved in, making a slow scraping sound on the hardwood floor.

Sitting down carefully between Stephan and Tomas, the floor beneath them was creaking from age and wear.

Once Brandon was quietly in place and the floor was no longer making the creaking sound, Nicolae intoned:

"Welcome Brandon, let me tell you a bit about us and then perhaps you could tell us a bit about yourself." Brandon brightened up as Nicolae started.

"We are indeed a Coven if you will; our interest, for several generations, has been beyond us in the darker aspects of Magick…we hold no Judeo-Christian ties, no prayers from the Key of Solomon or any such text. For those who do not believe in Magick, this could be a useless board game club for all that people care…" Nicolae continued.

"I have researched the foundation of this religion in my studies in the Middle East, specifically in Iran and in Syria. You must understand, the volume of our information has grown tenfold in the past five years." As Nicolae spoke with a commanding presence, Brandon noticed that the others gave more than respectful attention.

Nicolae grew silent, staring at Brandon; this must be his cue, he thought quickly.

"I have been a student of Crowley, practiced with some Lodges in the USA in the past, Anton LaVey is of course interesting as well. I have looked for something new and interesting for some time, I truly wish for initiation into a darker group…not just the ideological "Satanists" and so forth. I think Magick is a means of expanding the mind, the power of the self…" Brandon could only stop for a few seconds to catch his breath, his mind racing with ideas he wanted to share with them.

"So you should know we are not a 'white light' group", Anton stated firmly without a smile.

"Of course, that is why I became interested, after the bookstore clerk told me about you."

"Which bookstore, if you don't mind me asking?" Tomas, sitting next to him chimed inquisitively.

"The World of Wisdom it is called, I cannot remember the name of the clerk." Brandon said looking at Nicolae.

"I know of it; I have been to that store before…" Tomas said in what appeared to be a strong Swedish accent. Several others nodded their heads in agreement.

"Our Magick is based around Azathoth, H.P. Lovecraft's title, you see. Except," Nicolae carefully stated, "Lovecraft knew what he wrote was not only fiction".

"I have spent many years outside of Romania; the Ceausescu regime was a challenge to us; I returned in 1991, a few years after the regime had ended. It can still be very chaotic here at times…A very useful place for us." Nicolae mentioned.

"Can you imagine that with a serious working pattern in ritual, you can actually communicate with something such as a series of powerful spirits?" Nicolae looked in awe while asking with a proud, hidden, and an almost sinister undertone.

"I think that would be amazing!" Brandon exclaimed.

No one is smiling…the café's room is filled and loud, lowering Brandon's anxiety despite the fact that the others were no longer smiling…if the Dante were empty, it would be much more awkward.

"Are you familiar with ceremonial Magick, actually performing or just reading about?" Anton raising an eyebrow, only now while slightly smiling.

"I have performed many of Crowley rituals, Liber Samekh and such". Brandon chimed.

"We take Magick very seriously, we do not look upon it as parlor tricks; our goal is to *Cross the Threshold,* as it is named…everything in this world and the next has barriers; we just have to find the way to cross it or to make the barriers cross over…you understand?" Nicolae explained.

"Yes, I think so." Brandon replied, his mind now racing with ideas...is this guy for real? Do they really believe they will do this? *I have to see this myself*, Brandon thought to himself.

"Good, you will have your chance to experience this…when do you go back to America?" Erzsebet mentions, her English a little more understandable than her partners'.

"I have two weeks or so left; I am a web designer so I am able to work from virtually anywhere." Brandon smiles as he quickly recalled those years of working a menial job while he was going to school - how much more freedom he has now.

"Monday evening, I will give you an address to go to. Don't worry about robes, you will be fine." Nicolae mentions as he begins writing on the back of a napkin.

"I look forward to it, thank you for allowing me"

"Monday night, 8 PM, come alone of course – my number is on the back" Nicolae interrupts.

"Good night then, I look forward to it" Brandon no longer smiling, knowing full well it is his cue to leave.

Walking to the hotel, Brandon feels the darkness heavier than before, almost as if he is to be a part of something he should not be.

What a feeling….

NIGHT

Waking up, Brandon rubbed his eyes and was quick to gather his senses despite the darkness of the night. He heard so many sounds it felt as if he was in a forest, surrounded by insects and other crawling night creatures. Looking around, it was as if reality was trying to keep up: everything was slower than usual. Just as he perceived this, Brandon began to think about the strangeness...

Once Brandon stood up, everything appeared to be back to normal. It is dark, no insects or noises other than the usual night sounds of a city. Brandon, near the bed itself, took a deep breath and carefully put on a t-shirt and some jeans. While sitting down to put on his jeans, he felt the bed sink slightly, accompanied by the sound of a small creak in the metal frame of the bed. Pulling up his dark blue jeans, Kestle quickly buttoned them while walking to the door with almost clumsy steps. He feels an itch on his left shoulder and attempts to scratch it while touching the door knob.

While opening the hotel room door, a slight creak echoes through the hallway. Hearing this, Brandon quietly closes his door and is able to see quite well in the dark, even though he woke up in the middle of the night. As he walks to the restroom at the end of the hallway, he eagerly goes inside and closes the door ever-so quietly.

Once inside the restroom and facing the mirror, Brandon flips the light switch and the initial flood of light blinds him.

After overcoming the blinding light, starting from a tense squint, Brandon slowly opens his eyes to see his face.

With bluish veins, his pallor is a one-day dead ghost-white. His eyes are a burning black and inset. A plethora of flies are looming right above and behind his left shoulder. With too many flies to count, in a sense of shock from his appearance, Brandon attempts to smack the flies away with his right hand. He now turns his face towards the mirror, no longer frightened to take a look at his shoulder. He inspects his shoulder by moving the collar on the hunter-green t-shirt away from his neck far enough to expose his bare shoulder. What Brandon finds next causes him to panic and move fast towards the door as if jumping out of the way of something.

There is a tear in his skin, the wound appears infected, it is bright red around it with a black liquid seeping out of it, possibly old blood, yet it appears to look like motor-oil. He felt a hostile push from the wound, followed by a sharp pain. From the wound emerged a single hair-covered insect leg - it moved to touch the surface of his shoulder and insects continued to emerge from the open wound. In his head, Brandon heard the voices and blaring sound of the insects around the room.

"Come to us child, we have been waiting in the dark, sleeping like the dead, come in the name of the blackened one."

With a sudden jerk, Brandon sat up suddenly in his bed. Sweating and stunned, he summoned the spark to reach over and pick up his phone, checking the time. 4:02 AM – all is calm - just a nightmare.

Not like any he has ever had.

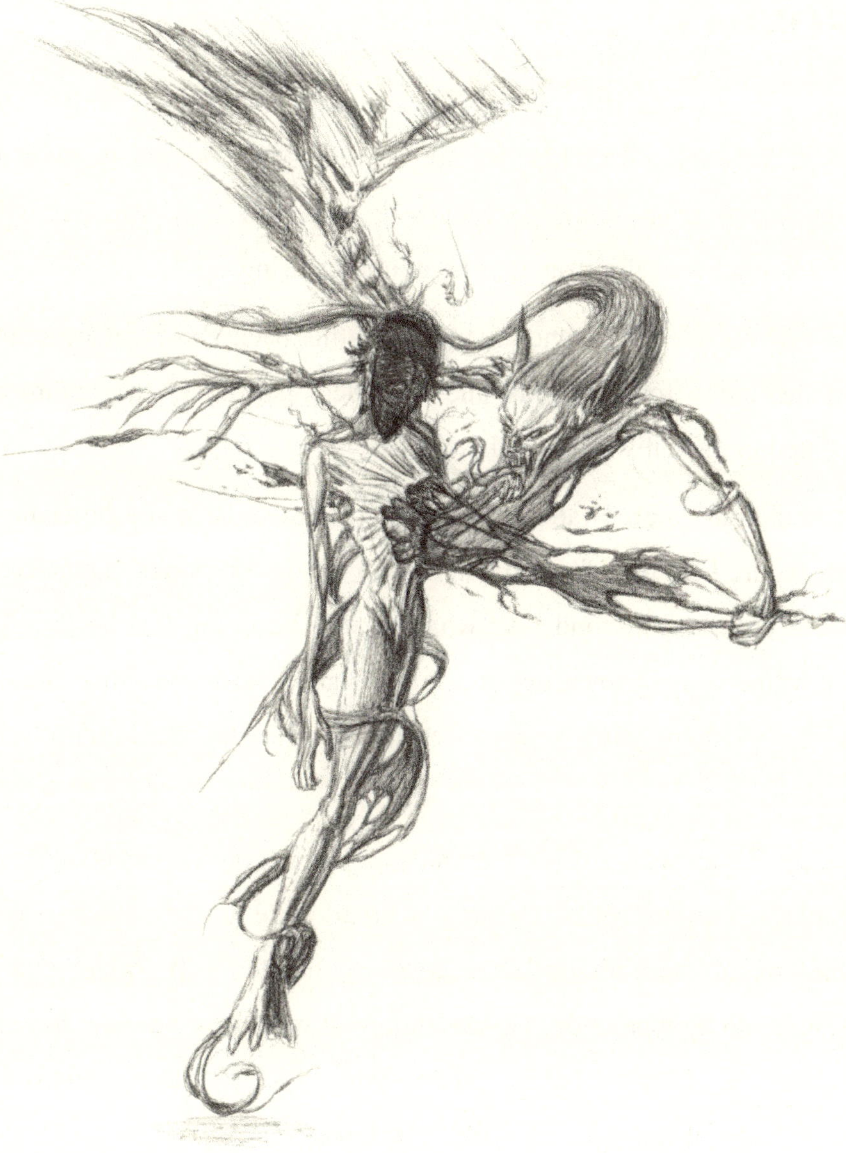

MONDAY

The sunlight was shining through the worn and faded blinds in the hotel, Brandon raises himself up; an old t-shirt he has worn many nights before is scratched…knowing that his day will end with something hopefully strange is no doubt inspiring.

Rolling out of bed, Brandon straightens his back slowly as he stands up, he looks for his pants and considers getting to the bathroom, located in the hallway of the hotel.

A half hour later, Brandon enters the street outside the hotel he is staying in. Feeling refreshed and new to the day, he looks inquisitively down both ways, wondering what he will be doing for the day. He knows he wants to rest up later, but does not want too much time to think; else he may invoke some tension which will make him not want to show up.

Clean shaven with a black button down shirt, a brown jacket and dark slacks, Brandon walks towards a small café to get lunch. He is thinking of the Cult he has become acquainted with, what type of Magick do they practice? He was hoping it would not be some pseudo-Satanic or Chaos Magick group, whose ideas lacked depth and knowledge, it was wanting…like a bad date.

7:28 PM – MONDAY EVENING

Walking in the brisk twilight evening, Brandon grew excited, almost as if he could not fully catch his breath. Looking down at the napkin with the address on it, he was counting on it not being a worthless experience - all day he was concerned with it – what a waste of time it would be if he could not redeem the time he was spending thinking about it.

Brandon stood in front of a dilapidated building, which by the looks of it, was so old, it was just a few years away from being reduced to a dump. The six windows in the front of the building were painted black, he noticed; "Nice touch" he thought.

The doors were sliding, two large brown doors which looked as if they could no longer fit and close correctly. Brandon eagerly tapped the left door, one…two…three… and waited.

He could not hear anything at first, and then a few seconds later he heard faint voices; he could not make out any English; they approached the door at last with only one voice present.

Hearing a type of lock mechanism, the right door slid open slowly, creaking and revealing a seeming warmth within. Already relieved, Brandon smiled wide as he was greeted by Nicolae, who was adorned in a hooded crimson robe, the hood itself not pulled up. The lady behind him, Erzsebet, was dressed in a plain black robe.

"Welcome Mr. Kestle, please come in…" Nicolae expressed warmly with a slight smile.

"Thank you, a very interesting building from what I see." Brandon remarked.

"It suits our needs, that is for sure…good to see you again Mr. Kestle." Erzsebet smiled almost seductively as she took his hand.

The walls, painted gray have a greenish tint to them, like a slight moss or perhaps mold – although it does not smell like mildew. The old fashioned light on the wall gives off a yellow – 1970's flare.

To the left in an at least 10 year old frayed green fabric chair – sat a little girl in a red dress. She had brown hair in two pigtails at the side of her head, her fair smile and green eyes really set him at ease – nothing strenuous where there is a little girl, Brandon thought to himself.

"This is my daughter, Viktoria." Erzsebet looked at her with a careful smile, almost with a respect of sorts.

"Hi there." Brandon chimed and bowed forward a bit to reach her level.

She just smiled and nodded her head.

"Please come with us, I would like to prepare you for the working by giving some background information on our work and how you will assist us." Nicolae said flatly.

"Yes of course"…Brandon remarked as Nicolae wasted no time in leading the way. Erzsebet walked behind Brandon…she watched his movements, his statue and posture, then quickly looked down.

At the end of the hallway was a single door, the walls were cracked, white, with a single light bulb in the middle of the hallway. It seems the walls were painted many years ago, now aged and almost a slight yellow, some of the paint was peeling away. The door, a stone gray, was at the end of a hallway of nine feet in height. Nicolae opened the door inward which revealed a candlelit room…although it felt colder stepping into the room than it was in the hallway.

The walls in this large room were painted a fresh glossy black, they seemed to shine in their grandeur, different sections were painted over with large murals….horrifying and demonic. There were pale skeletal figures drinking blood from young women, a crimson outlined figure, which was a dull black, with two burning yellow eyes. There were strange sigils outlined on the walls which were twisted like spiders, their shapes giving the impression of a sinister aspect connected with them.

The ceiling of the room was a bright red, like a sea of blood above them all.

"A beautiful fucking room." Brandon blurted out in awe; these people are really into this, he thought…so much effort to decorate.

The room was crowned by an altar at the wall opposite to the door, with a large tile bathtub (for a lack of a better word) in front of it.

"What is this used for?" Brandon asked Nicolae who was nearing the altar.

"It is for our higher degree sexual rites…" Nicolae replied smiling slightly.

"I see." Brandon began to think to himself: "Another fuck-club, amazing…", he did not come to Romania for a sex club…although the women are pretty hot…Brandon cleared the thought from his mind.

The six in the room were all cloaked in black except for Nicolae, who wore a beautiful crimson robe. The altar was a large pedestal obviously used in Catholic rites some years back, or something similar. A large inverted cross was attached to the center of the pedestal.

"The inverted cross, a symbol of ascension from the faith of weakness, we are not Christians as you must know." Erzsebet chimed to Brandon, looking at the altar with a raised eyebrow.

"Babylonian spirits know time and understand the enemies of the day. No longer shall they fear Marduk, now it is some of the Christians who can call their so-called light against them." Nicolae explained.

The top of the altar was a large, plain, but black mirror. A sigil was painted directly below it.

On the altar sat a silver chalice, as Brandon drew closer to it, he noticed there were herbs or something similar within it, yet no liquid.

"This is a cult or group dedicated to Azathoth, a God of Magick. Tonight you will see for yourself Mr. Kestle; may I call you Brandon?" Nicolae asked.

"Yes, please…" Brandon replied, curious as to what Nicolae was telling him.

"Azathoth is not a Satanic group *per se*, we are exclusively dedicated to He of the Darkness, the shadow which makes flesh white…eyes burn and throat thirsty….you shall see", chuckling Nicolae said.

"You will be the seventh in our group….much like the symbolism of ancient Babylonia, or later the corrupt Judeo-Christians, the Dragon represents power of the number. Calling forth the essence of Azathoth requires seven." Erzsebet said with an underlining sense of excitement.

"We have accomplished communion with Azathoth before." Tomas said looking wide eyed to Brandon.

"What type of phenomena have you experienced?" directing his question to Tomas.

"Shadows, a type of voice appearing in our heads, telling us of preparation, that we can be immortal…we painted the walls based on these communications." Nicolae informed Brandon.

"Our book is old; I have had it in my family's possession for years…it was my Grandfathers. He studied Magick with others; he transcribed ancient Egyptian and Sumerian tablets and cuniform texts from which he wrote this grimoire. He did not finish it however, he died before he could." Nicolae explained.

Displaying the book to Brandon, it was larger than 8 X 11 in size, bound in old brown leather; the same sigil, the sign of Azathoth, was inscribed in red on the cover.

"For this ritual, you will wear the black robe and focus on the mirror, it is a gateway my friend." instructed Nicolae.

"You see, Chal-dean in origin, there were said to be many tablets R.C. Thompson did not publish, many which were too much for the Christian world then"..Nicolae lit up with bright eyes and assumed a more comfortable tone and posture.

His hand touched the shoulder of Brandon, while explaining intently.

"You see, the Asakki Marutti series produced some incantations which spoke of Azathoth and the Worm, which many thought was related to toothache and disease – this was not so! You see, The Worm is a serpent or dragon in Babylonian Mythology, it had an unquenchable thirst for blood, and in one actual published tablet, went to a "god" and asked it for blood." Nicolae continued.

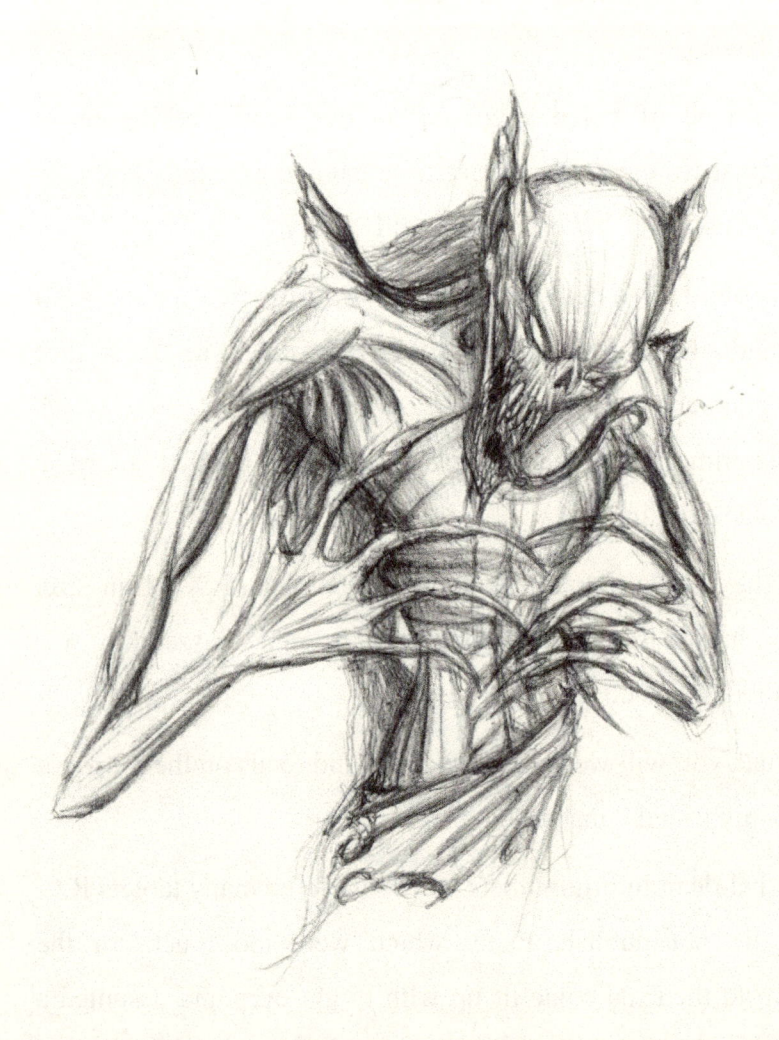

"I have seen it and have translations of the other tablets; we incorporate them into our works now. The Worm is something so real, it is a Vampire, yet at the same time it will empower the practitioners and give them something of immortality. Very hard to believe, is it not? We are the children of this darkened chaos, like the Babylonian myth of Tiamat and Kingu – his blood was used to make us."

Nicolae peered into Brandon's eyes with a growing intensity – a type of cunning smile now showing on his lips. Brandon understood this was not a fucking gothic ritual but something at the primal base of humanity – to devour or be devoured.

"Let's do what others have not had the knowledge to do – we will open their gates here and now..."

"You may think this is funny, no, better yet, how do you say in America, stupid – just humor us Brandon." Nicolae said slowly "I can tell you the experience will be shocking, something that will make you wish to run, but refrain from doing so."

Brandon slowly raised his head to look Nicolae directly in the eyes; "I fully intend to follow this through.", Thinking more of the cold than reassuring him about his intent to stay.

"Good then, let's begin." Nicolae responded, "Time is not a factor, this rite just has to be conducted at night." the accent of his voice ringing a more distinct European flavor than Bela Lugosi. Stephan handed Brandon a robe which he took in his hands respectfully. He walked slowly over to the door area while the others lit candles, he put the robe on, closing it with a knotted clasp; the robe had a crushed black velvet texture like the ones worn by the others.

Three members stood on one side, three others including Brandon on the other, all facing the altar. There was no sound in the chamber, no ritual music recordings or anything to create the moon.

It was dead silent.

Candles lit, burning black near the altar, the reflection dull into the black mirror. "What type of altar piece is a black mirror?" Brandon thought. This is like the Greeks and how they practiced necromancy in their caves and places ages ago. The mirror itself was a bizarre shape, sinister in appearance – the frame was a bit off, like an elongated face with jagged peaks near the top.

It was so cold in this room…Brandon thought, he could see the slight breaths of the others. It was literally getting colder in here, it is happening so slowly that no one can notice. This defiantly adds to the experience Brandon thinks to himself.

The chanting began…slow, droning voices…they have done this before, Brandon knew it. They were dead on…*AZ-A-THOTH…AZ-A-THOTH*….one voice was almost guttural. It sounded like Tibetan chanting.

Knowing only a trivial amount about the supposed "Babylonian Demons", Brandon knew that they would prove to be entertaining, to say the least. He did not really appreciate the seriousness of the others but respected their aim and intent. He chose to perform the rite with them with full vigor.

"By the Darkness come forth, By the Earth come forth!" Nicolae intoned with brooding intensity.

"ZAZAS ZAZAS NASATANADA ZAZAS!" Erzsebet and Nicolae shouted, over and over again.

"We gather here, spit at the image of Marduk! We, children of Azathoth laugh at the blindness of the Light of Marduk! We curse those forces which betray Tiamat, our Mother! We laugh at the failed priests who have not managed to lock out our darkness! Let nothing shield us, children of the black sun. We call thee forth Nyarlathotep, hidden darkness, messenger of chaos!"

The candles burnt in the chamber with a light which seemed unreal. It actually started to turn a ghostly blue, which caused immediate alarm to him – it was bloody real!

The evocations continued, the atmosphere in the room was very strange, almost other-worldly.

At the end of the evocation, Nicolae went forth to the altar and took the chalice in his hand, along with a small knife he had in his robe already.

The Black Mirror seemed to exude shadow and smoke from it, as if faces were appearing and in the same instant disappearing. Brandon was not too concerned about the dagger at this point, he was simply exhilarated at the smoke and the presence in the room – it was like a great rush!

Nicolae went first to Erzsebet who held the chalice at waist level. Her eyes could not be seen as the black hood was over her head slightly. Nicolae raised his wrist and cut his arm ever slightly – the blood soon began to drip in the chalice at a few-drops-a-moment. Nothing horrifying really, after all, blood sacrifice had been done since the dawn of humanity…

Once Nicolae has bled into the chalice, he then handed the knife to Erzsebet and then took the chalice in his hand while she cut herself gently. He could see the start of a grimace on her face.

Each member repeated this process, passing down slowly until reaching Brandon.

Brandon wiped the blade on his robe before cutting himself gently at the tip of his forefinger on the left hand. He bled into the cup, noticing the blackened contents which appeared to have insects moving about in it. Brandon was growing a bit sick of this situation – Nicolae was eager to take the chalice away from his hand and to face the altar.

He raised his arms and chanted something which must have been in ancient Sumerian.

His fevered pitch rose as he invoked the Daemon Azathoth. At the end of the invocation, the black mirror suddenly became manifested with three cracks – shattered! The mirror shards exploded out as everyone turned away to avoid it. Nicolae had not been so lucky - a piece of mirror cut his right cheek. After wiping it away, he looked to all of the participants, knowing they were shaken as well.

Brandon looked up and noticed that where the mirror once was, there is a seeming pit of darkness going into the wall – or where the wall should be, the air in the room seemed to twist and move against all within it, like a vortex.

"I have to get the fuck out of here, this can't be good" Brandon thought, panicking.

He raced for the door yet noticed great black shapes rushing forth from the abyssic area in the wall. He was knocked down by a gust of wind or some force he that had no shape. Hitting the floor hard, it had slightly knocked the wind out of him. Brandon looked over with his head down and could see multitudes of black shapes entering the participants. These black shadows had no forms yet he could hear a howling coming from them. The room pulsated with aggression. The shadows attacked the bodies of the members by entering them, due to which their bodies convulsed and fell to the floor one by one. Nicolae and Erzsebet went over to the tub, the black shadows were following them yet not attacking – very odd.

Feeling like he was overlooked, forgotten for the moment or whatever, Brandon crawled towards the door. It was as if the black shadows could not sense him. The sound of rushing wind in the room was now complicated with a sound of what appeared to be distant flutes – droning.

Now within reach of the door, Brandon was ready to rise and run. He glanced over and saw Erzsebet leaning over the tub, blood pouring from her throat – Nicolae was backing up towards the abyss which had opened in the wall. Nicolae suddenly looked over as if trying to see through the darkness.

"The seventh, look to the door, the SEVENTH"! Nicolae screamed in panic, his robe nearly torn away from his neck, blood splattered his face as the abyssic gateway opened through the mirror; it enveloped Brandon and began entering him with violent thrusts.

Brandon did not wait – he slammed into the door, turning the knob.

The howling continued as he slid those old brown doors open as he hit the street. He tore off the robe and ran. There were not many out tonight. He could give a fuck less if he shut those doors. Sweating, pale and grateful to be able to escape that hell, Brandon just ran until exhaustion overtook him, from then on he could only walk quickly.

Where was the little girl? Brandon did not see her anywhere but he was not exactly looking for her either. "Should I go to the police? They'll lock me up or deport me…" He kept running.

Arriving at his hotel, out of breath, exhausted and scared, Brandon went into his room, closing the door and resting against it.

Trying to catch his breath, many thoughts raced through his mind. He held up his cell phone, yet had no idea who to call.

A new message – it was a text of all things.

He opened the message and a simple line "U dont leave when u must stay"

It was from Nicolae

Brandon went over to his bed and fell on it, just wanting to forget it.

The sleep of darkness came quickly, Hypnos was merciful that evening.

3:00 AM - TUESDAY MORNING

A white face, black eyes, cracked lines or veins under the surface of the skin. Lips cruel and sensual, opening to reveal curved and perverse fangs, blackened and clotted blood dripping out, a forked tongue...I can hear the blackened finger nails dancing across the window, scraping and scratching....

Waking in nightmare sweat, Brandon sat up trying desperately to catch his breath. He felt as if he was drowning...you know what they say about those who die drowning in their sleep...they don't wake up. Picking up the cell phone, he checked for messages – nothing but a low battery.

Falling back into bed, Brandon's mind raced with options – go back to the place to see if it all really happened...going back to the States and forgetting about it for a while...hell, how could you forget *that*?

7:25 AM – TUESDAY MORNING

Waking, groggy, light peering through the window. Brandon could see the streaks on the glass, like finger prints or greasy hands which touched the window. He could also see what appeared to be lines in some dark substance on the glad, four of them with smudge marks on the glass near the window lock.

Moving the off-white sheet off and away from his legs, Brandon moves with a sense of urgency towards the window.

What a vacation.

Looking at the window glass up close, it appeared to be dried blood and the streaks on the window seemed to be actually ingrained or cut into the glass with something razor-sharp. They were sleek and sharp, cut in the movement of four fingers.

There was just one streak, with smudges of blood slightly below the window lock, as if something had tried to open the window from there. There was more to that nightmare than he had considered.

Heart racing faster, he could no longer stand it. Had to go and see for himself.

8:12 AM – TUESDAY MORNING

After a brief shower and fresh clothes, he was downstairs to pay for another day. After the obligatory pleasantries, Brandon left to go back to the place where this nightmare started. Although Brandon usually starts his day with a cup of coffee, he forgot about it this morning until he got about half way there. He needed some caffeine, so much pain today already – last night had played hell on his nerves. A small café gave him the edge he needed, no to-go cups here so he was fast to drink the strong coffee down.

9:22 AM - TUESDAY MORNING

Arriving in front of those old double brown doors – they were closed. Brandon gripped the handle of the right-side of the door with both hands firmly and slid it open. Surprised that it was not locked, the old door slid with the same reluctance of the previous evening. Heart racing, sweat forming on the brow, Brandon attempted to peer into the darkness of the building and he looked into the front room with a sense of panic near the surface of his controlled calm.

The calm would not be shaken…nothing jumped at him, yet as he hesitantly walked into the room, he grew uneasy at the feeling of something else watching him. Brandon did not actually see anything peculiar, the light from the previous evening was on and the room looked messy – like a storm had gone through it.

Something smelled in the place, like an animal that had died in the wall or somewhere in the corner. It was not horrid quite yet, but it was like something dead was nearby.

With each step Brandon felt his breathing grow heavy, like his heart was beating out of control, he felt as if anything nearby could hear it. Loosing himself in the fear, he turned around once he gained his senses and slowly pulled the door nearly closed. Not quite all the way, just in case he had to run quickly.

Not knowing what awaited him, he walked forward towards the overturned chair where Viktoria was sitting the night before. The floor around the chair seemed to have some dried blackish substance on the floor. Looking ahead and around, Brandon kneeled in a half-hearted attempt to investigate the substance on the floor.

Taking his forefinger, Brandon rubbed it along the substance but it was already dried.

Rising to his feet and with a deep cautious breath, Brandon went forward to the closed door which led to the warehouse room which was used as the ritual chamber the night before.

Brandon opened the door with hesitant caution, looking in to see absolutely no light. Remembering the location of the light switch from the night before, Brandon was able to enter the room, casting a shadow in the lit area from the still burning light from the entry room. Brandon went forward to the right and felt along the wall to turn on the light switch.

He flipped the bottom switch and nothing happened. With a frightened hand he moved it upward to the switch above. Brandon felt what could have been spider legs, but so many.

Not able to see it in the complete darkness shadowed by the entry room light, a fiendish shadow, a twisted face, pale white and streaked in what could have been black oil, spider legs emerging from the darkened mass of its body, hanging along the wall. It looked at Brandon with pitch black eyes, tongues flickering out of its mouth and smelling him – its spider-like legs touching his hand in the moment before the light came on.

With the flick of the switch, darkness banished the fiend non-existence.

The large oblong room was drenched in dried blood mixed with streaks of that blackened liquid over it and several puddles could be seen in other places. There was a stench about the room which was like something old and long dead. While Brandon could not quite place it, he knew the stench was not there the previous night.

Staring directly at the shattered mirror at the altar, it looked like it had been abused beyond belief. Broken glass scratched and chipped frame already worn from a strange and almost surreal construction. The angles which composed the frame were just plain strange.

The wall, which was behind it, was just the slick and glossy black wall. Last evening, it was a gateway for the abyss – now just a wall. "This did happen." Brandon thought, the blood…the smell that is here now.

Looking over to the bath tub which Nicolae had described as being used for "sex rites", Brandon noticed that it had now actually been covered in dried blood.

The scene raced through his mind again, Erzsebet bleeding profusely from her throat, leaning over the tub while Nicolae stood there, in all the madness and now before him, nothing. Stains and a fuzzy, almost surreal memory of the previous night along with a strange text message to end it all, that's the situation.

Suddenly, the lights flickered in the room. They went off briefly and in that moment Brandon had wished he had stayed near his hotel.

Before his eyes, dropping down in the moment of pitch black darkness, a face pale white with blood crusted over it in streaks – showed a waxy and almost mask-like quality of what could have been a man. He recognized the face but could not place it. The teeth were all sharp and cruel, like an alligator or some type of reptilian beast – open and dripping blackened blood over him. The eyes were abyssic pools of darkness, without human emotion. The head of this beast, hanging down from the ceiling with spider legs, yet larger, danced around the skull. They were moving, insect-like near the head, moving forward towards Brandon as he stood there in that instant – speechless. The moustache, which was barely visible by the amount of blackened blood on it, and the razor-sharp fangs took precedence as the most noticeable features on the face. This looked just "like" Nicolae – a horrific vision of Nicolae that is!

Brandon backed up as the lights returned to normal, slamming into the altar and causing the mirror to sway back and forth a bit. Brandon looked down near the tub next to the altar and with a quick sweep of his hand picked up the grimoire they had used last night. It was discarded, forgotten about in the chaos.

Sweating and shaken, Brandon left again quickly not turning off the light switch as he went out.

Going out of the building, he closed the sliding door and went off as fast as he could without appearing like a freak to the people out and about. He kept the book close to him as he walked.

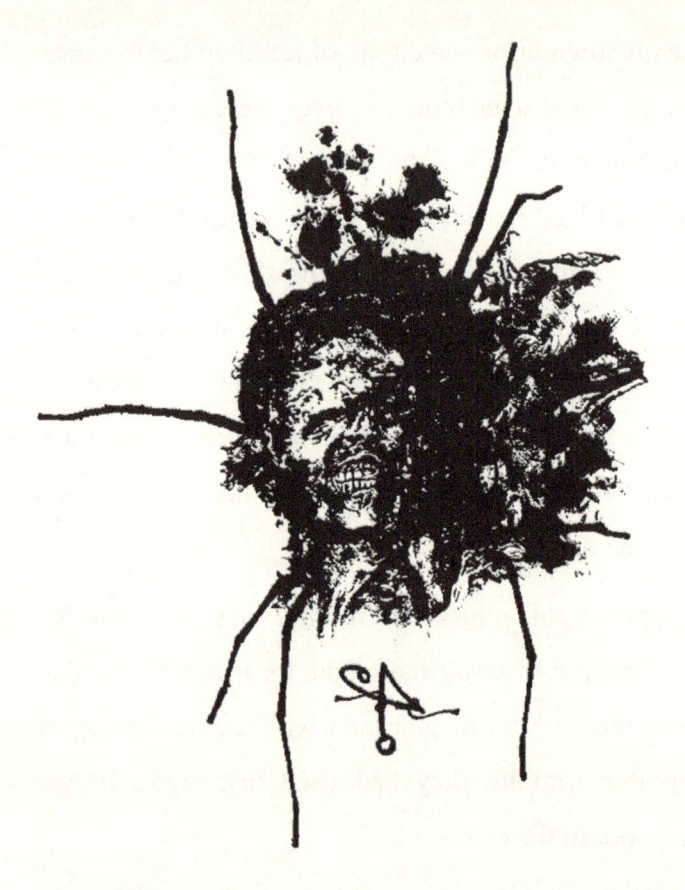

2:30 PM - TUESDAY AFTERNOON

Arriving back at the hotel, the clouds had really overcast. What was to be a very hot day was now very windy and growing colder by the hour. Storms must be rolling in.

Entering his hotel room, Brandon went in and shut the door carefully, locking it at once. He sat on the edge of his bed, looking now at the cover of that worn leather cover with the strange symbol in the leather. He was told it was "Azathoth" by Nicolae. Opening the cover he saw drawings in black ink of shadow-like beings, symbols he knew were "sigils" or fingerprints of the beings of the otherworld, and words inscribed in Latin and actual English – which pleased him. The grimoire must have been passed down through many generations.

THE BOOK OF THE AZATHOTH

A Tome of the Calling of the Hungering Ones

The title page was haunting, AZATHOTH – what was it? Brandon had read of it before in various manuscripts, yet he was not aware of actual cults and practices surrounding it. It seems partly Egyptian and also Babylonian. Reading onward, the grimoire was indeed in English and not Romanian or another language associated with Nicolae.

"Understand now, those who offer callings into the veiled darkness of the abyss. Shall the vampires composed of hungering shadow, see the devil-dancing flames from our world, will be drawn to them...they shall seek the gateway you call a mirror and break forth into our world."

He eagerly continued his reading, carefully flipping page by page...

"Like a tree planted the shades of Azathoth, thou burning hunger of the abyss, the Black Magickian whose lust for immortality made him a God in times long past, shall take root in this world of the living. Like a tree the roots are nourished in the dark, then with the blood or substance they continue to grow and multiply, devouring life according to the food chain of this physical world. The Vampire here is our predator – yet there is escape. Those who open gateways or make the path for Nyarlathotep to guide the dark ones here shall be embodied with the shades of the abyss, the vampire becoming one with the human until they are one hungering embodiment of the primal."

Heart racing, eyes dancing across the page, Brandon realized what he had assisted in – opening a literal gateway to hell. He read on, the descriptions, noted as being from Ancient Babylonia – a time plagued with vampires, demons and malicious Gods – a type of spirit which wandered the wastelands:

"A rushing hag-demon, she who drinks from the veins of children and sleeping women. It is the sickness of night and day, hiding where none would not look; Whose head is that of a demon, Whose shape is as the destroying Whirlwind; Its appearance is as the darkening heavens, its face as the deep shadow of the forest, biting down and draining of all vitality."

A type of Vampire, this Hag-Demon called "Labartu" obviously had many powers which enabled travel in the spirit world. Continuing on, Brandon studied the manuscript:

"To open the gate anew, there must be seven willing participants, for the dark gods have little time to enter this world and gain material form with the blood and spirit of another. Those who willingly give will join with these gods, they shall in part have their own history but

gain the memories of the timeless beings which embody them. This is the act of invocation, calling within the forces of darkness and becoming something 'else'"...

AZATHOTH

A Tome of the Calling of the Hungering Ones

Understand now, those who offer callings into the
veiled darkness of the abyss.
Shall the vampires composed of hungering shadow,
see the devil-dancing flames
from our world

"Like a tree planted the shades of Azathoth,
thou burning hunger of the abyss.

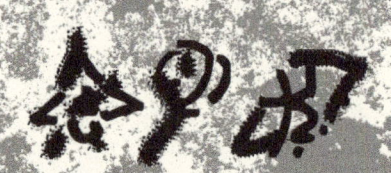

path for Nyarlathotep to guide the dark ones here shall
be embodied with the shades of the abyss

The seven are described:

"Seven are they, the seven gods of igneous spheres, the seven gods, the seven malevolent phantoms of the flames, the wicked demon, the wicked Gigim, the wicked Telal, the wicked Maskim, the Malevolent Eye.."

Brandon reads on, understanding that the seven are needed to embody physical hosts in the world; they enter the body and devour the blood – giving power to the darkness of their spirit-bodies, and then taking any perverse shape they wish from the flesh they have embodied. They are able to take action in darkness and when light touches them they are temporarily – he studies the word – temporarily harmless. If only temporarily, how could one stop them? *Who could even try?*

"They are seven, the first the shadow which takes the form of the beast

The second, the pestilence of wind-storm

The third, a leopard who bites deep into its prey

The Fourth, a serpent which strangles

The fifth, the ravening wolf who enters its prey

The sixth, the rebellious giant who was born of flame

The seventh, the messenger of the fatal wind called Namtar"

Azathoth would not appear per se in this world, yet sends forth children into the world. What is Nylarlathotep? Reading on: *"Nyarlathotep is the messenger of chaos, breeding phantoms in the world and directing their devouring actions. As such Vampires or Phantoms must continually feed to remain in this world – much like humans except for the fact they drink the blood and sometimes eat the flesh of their prey. Essentially they must also absorb the spirit – energy of the one they feed from, devouring their spirit."*

Flipping to another page, Brandon studied the text despite the dried blood on this section:

AZAG-HUL – The Feast of The Shades

"Enter ye the flesh, O Messangers of Azathoth – may Nyarlatothep arrange thy passage. Once the seven have taken bodies they are free in the world. They shall feed and cleanse the world one by one, victim by victim, and through bodies cause wars and violence – bringing them more energy to embody."

"There were not Seven, I got away" Brandon thought to himself. Nicolae…was he Nyalathotep, did that demon dwell in him? That was the face he saw…spider like, yellowing fangs.

Brandon continued to look through the grimoire…what had he got himself involved in?

"Once entered into the world from their death-like sleep, the Shades of Azathoth are able to travel by the nightmares of other – in the dark of night. Such daemons are able to manifest or appear in the physical plane as night increases, they drink blood or by eating flesh they gain a longer time in our plane. Once dawn arrives, they must go back into the darkness and await time to enter again."

"Crossing the threshold allows the participants freedom from the abyss in which they opened".

Brandon felt the pulse of his phone and reached into his pocket to see who it was. Another text message. "B..come back to meeting place..explain ltr"

The number it was sent from is unknown.

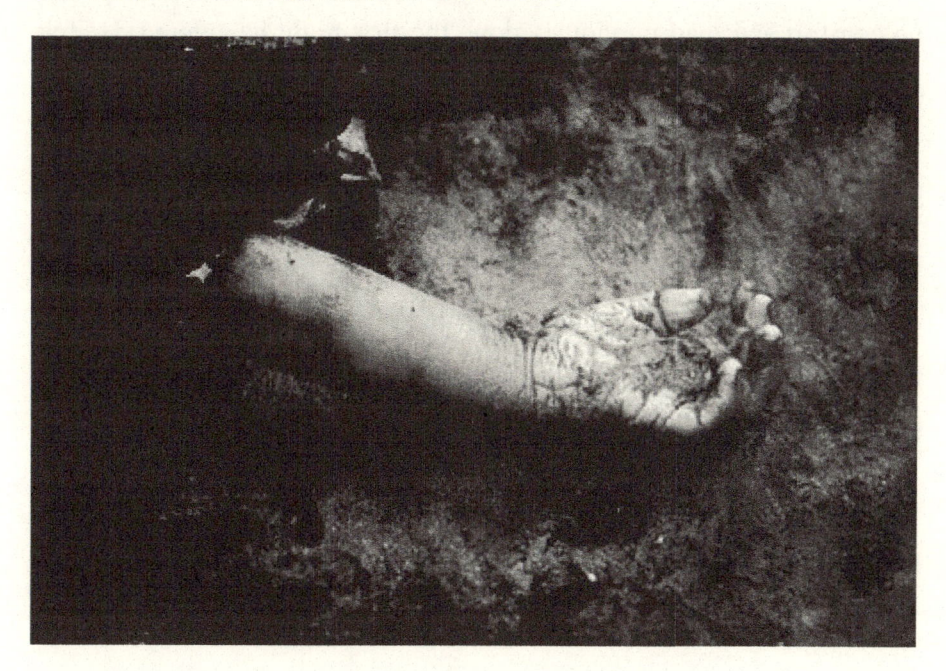

4:45 PM – TUESDAY AFTERNOON

Brandon moves towards the building once more, growing more cautious each step of the way, and filled with more forlorn than before. It was as if he knew it was a horrible idea – let's phrase it as plain stupid, yet he felt compelled to do so.

The sky above, despite the earlier wind picking up, continued to grow with storm clouds, as if something *knew* Mr. Kestle was walking closer, approaching the building in which the ghastly rites had been previously performed.

Sliding open the worn door yet again, Brandon cautiously stuck his head in and shouted a hearty "hello?" to which none replied. Almost relieved, Brandon entered and slowly closed the door. The light, still on in the entry room from his previous visit and the night before, gave no comfort as it had previously done the first night he entered. He felt strange, like being somewhere on a dare by his friends – he felt as if he was going to get caught doing something, even though he was not actually doing anything bad.

Brandon again shouted "hello!" with more force, his right hand clutching his American faded jeans as he did so. Too much coffee today had caused over-reaction to nearly everything. He needed nothing to help him "jump".

At once he heard several voices in unison – at the exactly the same moment, giggling like a small child, a little girl and several adults "Come in Brandon".

Brandon jumped; sweat forming on his brow, a cold chill overtaking his body. His eyes wide, wondering if he had only imagined it.

"Come in here…we have been waiting"…said the voice of a little girl. Was it Viktoria, Erzsebet's child?

Outside, the sounds were not any more comforting: thunder and the sound of heavy rain. While he could not actually see lightning due to the doors being closed and the windows being painted black, he could just imagine that lightning was flashing. Brandon started to walk towards the chamber room, knowing he had to satisfy this perverse curiosity he possessed.

Any normal person would not still be in the area.

Yet normal people don't seek out Magick groups and get caught up in some fucked up shit like this.

Lightning flashes as the lights flicker out, thunder above…close. Faces in the darkness. They are so white, burning black eyes, mouths open with ravenous smiles. Their limbs…unspeakable. Not human, yet Brandon has seen them before; the participants of the rite.

"Come closer" a child and old woman at the same moment spoke louder, yet it came from behind him.

Turning around, Brandon felt his heart in his stomach.

An aged hag, she was about five foot two or so, nude, sagging breasts with blackened patches of skin, coarse hair covering her body in parts with what looked like the legs of flies, she had the things coming from her. She was looking down – white stringy hair, wrinkled skin and long twisted, black and cruel nails. She was a fucking corpse, like one who the mortician had forgotten about or was too fearful to touch.

Her face rose up and flies scattered, like they listened to her every thought, waiting for the command to do something else. Her eyes opened greenish with strong black streaks within – like a shattered mirror, and her body was the temple the darkness resided in.

She opened her mouth to reveal hideous sharp fangs – she spit out what appeared to be blackened blood – the stench was worse than death.

"We have been WAITING" she started calm, yet ended in a scream. Flies scatter and buzz around her in complete chaos.

"Nothing left, nothing more, come to me boy" the Hag reached out with her twisted corpse-like limbs. On the ceiling above her, Viktoria – blackened eyes, pale and blue veins under her skin, pigtails yet her dress covered in dried blood – she looks down at Brandon, upside down. Her small arms and legs are clinging to the ceiling like a spider or some type of insect. Moving in fast and rapid sideway motions, Viktoria's mouth drips black blood and she whispers something in a forgotten tongue.

Brandon backs into the room – the light still on from the previous evening.

The light bursts, darkness consumes the room. With a flick of the light he saw too much.

Things people should not even see in their worst nightmares…like an accident happening in slow motion, Brandon attempted to stop it all until the dark closed in.

Then panic…cannot breathe…the nothingness of sleep.

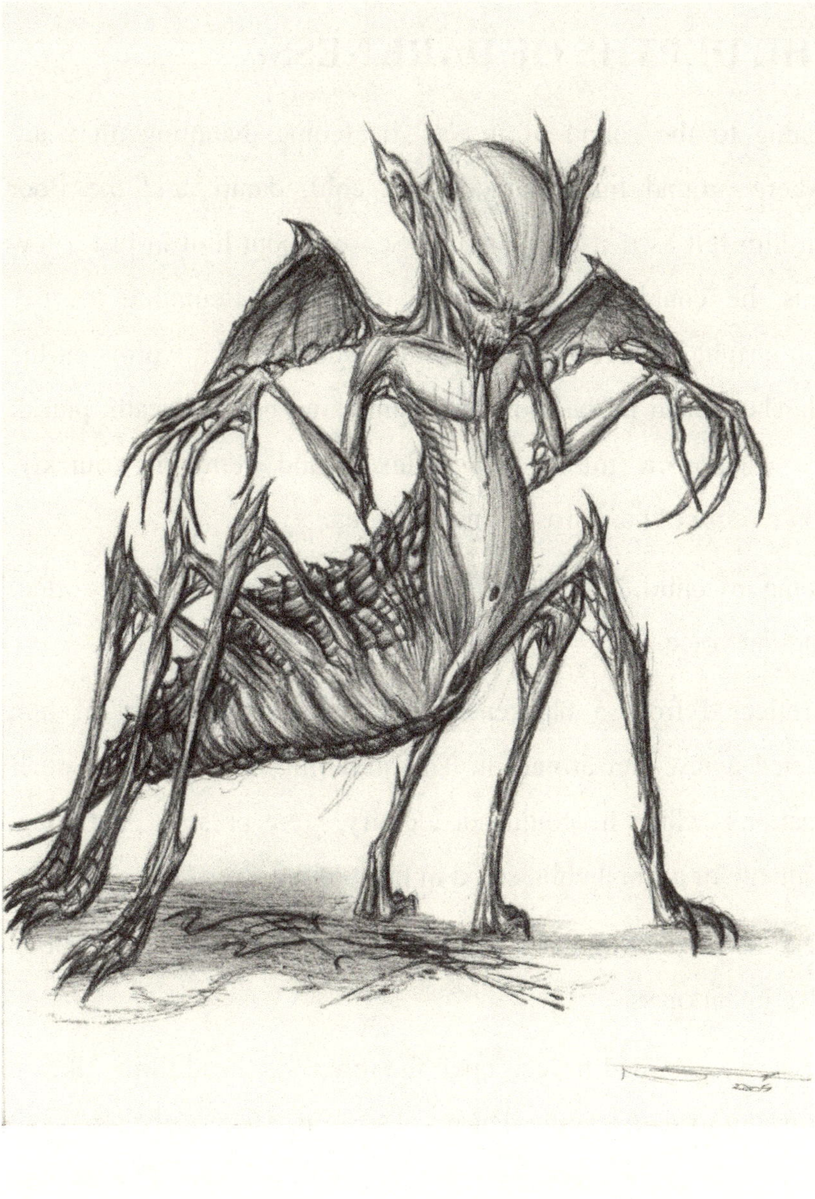

PART TWO:

IN THE DEPTHS OF DARKNESS

Awakening to the sound of insects, deafening, haunting: they are everywhere around him. Brandon felt cold, damp, and the floor beneath him felt as if it was moving. Senses about him in just a few moments, he could not see in front of him. Attempting to rise, Brandon's right hand reached down into what felt like worms on the ground. The stench in the room was something beyond death: putrid, initially causing a minor gag reflex. Hand retracting quickly, Brandon's sense of panic rose to new heights.

"Welcome my child, I am glad you came back to me" said a distorted, yet childlike voice.

Light reflected from a blackened mirror, a torch in front of him illuminated a few feet around it. The slithering of insects and other abominations, which he could not identify, were present. Scattering, the silhouette of a small child stood in front of the torch.

Darkness seemed to radiate around her, her frail and gentle body encircled in darkness.

Her black eyes seemed to feed upon the room, her head tilting like an animal trying to understand what was before it. She coughed and spit some black substance, and then insects began to spill out of her mouth. Her teeth bit down and Brandon cringed at the sounds of crushing and swallowing.

"Do you know what you have done, my young man?"…whispering around Brandon as he sat up, it was in one ear and then back to the dark somewhere else in the room.

"We have been liberated before; it is certainly not the *first* time. What is time anyway, we exist and move forward. This body serves me well for now, our shapes require nourishment, your blood, flesh…tears…although our spirit requires something else from your kind – your mind, your souls…" hissing, she stumbled forward…the little shell of the girl was lifted up off the ground by long and hair covered insect legs to a height of about one foot; Brandon kept his breath to try and stay calm.

The girl walked like she was a puppet pulled by someone not quite comfortable with controlling, the strings awkwardly moved so the limbs make insect-like sudden moves. She stands above Brandon, her clothes stained in what appears to be blood; she has, from what he can see, locusts and other insects on her face.

Slowly bending down her clawed hands, blackened at the tips where the nails are sharp and long like an animal, take him by the head, a vise-like grip which makes him shudder.

"Let me show you something, boy"…she whispers.

As she said this, Brandon's mind flooded with visions…. horrible… disgusting… he visualized something more real than any dream, his mother being consumed by insect-human hybrids, like they existed under the flesh and simply outgrew their human forms, they bit deep into his crying mother and were lapping up her blood… whimpering… His father was disemboweled and a smaller child-like corpse with black eyes carried the head away, chuckling and sucking on what could have been torn veins or muscles.

"Crossing the threshold allows the participants freedom from the abyss in which they opened."

Remembering this, Brandon, feeling broken, looked up towards the mirror and saw the girl-vampire looking down at him, emotionless. She let his head go; the pain it was causing was sharp and constant. Brandon knew that time was short; he was going to die…or worse.

The mirror continually manifested shadow-like faces, various things emerging, like coming from a dark-water pool under the veil of night.

"It is close to the time, child. You will join us; become one with us in spirit."

The sense of panic is not an easy sensation to master; thoughts overpowering other thoughts, the desire to run knowing you won't make it out. Brandon feels around on the floor and takes hold of a candle holder which fell during the previous ceremony. His hand tightened on it as firmly as he could muster, knowing that the monstrous abominations in this room could see him and his actions.

Hearing a rising and synched chanting, calls to the primordial gods of darkness were sounded and the room grew more oppressive. In a moment of complete desperation, Brandon, with all that he had left, threw the heavy candle stick holder with his right arm directly at the mirror which acted as a gateway to something worse. There was a crash and it seemed like everything in that room howled and rushed towards Brandon in that instant, and all consciousness was lost.

There was darkness…

AWAKENING

Head pounding, Brandon opened his eyes in the dark. There were no noises, horrid sounds, or smells beyond a slight putrid odor in the room. Realizing he was not dead, he began to sit up and felt no pain. He could see a slight light slithering through the edge of the doorway across the room, the only glare to even begin to cut into this darkness. With apprehension, he rose, not wanting to have anything touch him. Nothing did.

Stumbling slightly to the door, Brandon felt the blood rush from his head with a sudden sharp pain, much like a slight hangover or the feeling of dizziness when you stand up quickly after bending down. Brandon opened the door with a moving pace, wanting to know if he had really escaped all of this.

As the light engulfed and warmed his, skin Brandon squinted his eyes like never before. He began thinking, "Did I take something that night? Was this some strange trip?" yet he was never a drug taker really and he would certainly remember, unless it was slipped to him before or during the ritual. He didn't remember drinking anything given to him.

Walking slowly out into the lobby area, he felt his strength begin to come back to him; his head was slightly better and his pain had nearly left. With a bit of surprise, he saw the little Viktoria sitting in the same chair she was the first night he came to the place; she was wearing a brown dress in pigtails. What was even more striking was that she was perfectly normal, not the horrid insect girl the night before.

She smiled warmly, "hello" her English is decent, not a strong accent.

"Do you know where my mother is?" she chimed inquisitively.

"No....I can't say I do" Brandon replied, hesitantly.

"I found this..." Viktoria held out the Book of Azathoth....

"The pictures are very scary..." she said with a sense of fear.

Brandon felt his breath nearly stop, his skin went cold and he felt his heart racing.

"Can you take me home Mister? My mother lives not far…I want to go home and I have been here all day!"

All day Brandon thought. Had he truly been sleeping through most of the day?

"I have been sleeping, I think yesterday I came here, hiding from Mommie, but I fell asleep…sometimes she yells at me to clean with her, but I don't want to. I came here because I have been here many times, I know a secret way in and then I got scared to leave." Viktoria explained without hesitation.

"Sure, um, yes. Let's go then…" Viktoria gave the book to Brandon, who took it with hesitation.

Brandon could not find his cell phone… "My phone is missing; maybe I left it at my hotel room".

Sliding closed the large and very old brown door, twilight was approaching. The wind was light and it was a bit cold out. After ensuring the door was slid all the way closed, the two began walking the opposite way from which Brandon came. She held her hand out, looking up with a sweet glance of a little girl who needed guidance. Brandon reached out and held her hand without a word, just a smile. Viktoria's hand was very cold, he needed to get her home soon or she may get sick. Looking forward, both walked at a slight pace.

They went past a few people on the way: an older man, a younger couple – each looked at them with shock, nearly with disgust. Brandon thought to himself "they must either think I like little girls or I look like major crap today". Both kept walking and Brandon tossed it up to the previous night's black-out and the physical result of whatever they slipped him; these must have definitely caused some stress on his appearance.

MANOR

Brandon's mind raced at the images of his dream and looked down at the book he held in his left hand; he was hesitant at the thought of that nightmare being so real.

"Here!" Viktoria pointed at the two story home behind a black iron gate; the home appeared very old, standing up high to what appeared to be three stories; wooden-framed windows appeared to be at least 100 years old.

The seeming calm of the walk had ended with the confrontation of this manor as Brandon opened the unlocked gate before him, and allowing Viktoria to enter first. From the foreboding appearance of the manor, it looked like in the approaching night atmosphere that pale white faces peered out from the darkness of the high glass windows on the second floor, where curtains remained open.

The wind bit into his flesh as he walked through the gate, slowing behind Viktoria, who by posture alone appeared to be comfortable and at home. It is amazing what people can get used to, especially a small child.

As both approached the house, Brandon quipped with an optimistic smile and eyes squinting in the wind: "Well, do you have a key to get in?"

"The door is not locked, Mr. Kestle." Viktoria answered.

She turned towards him, not squinting really even against the air; she must be quite used to this weather.

"Come in please, I am a bit scared" she said with slow syllables, her hand reaching out innocently.

Brandon took a deep breath, instincts guiding him away from this, but he knew that it would be a travesty and spinelessness to leave a young child home without supervision, even if it was her home. He had not located her parents yet, from all the lights off in the house he was sure they were not home.

"Mother must be taking a nap; perhaps sleeping?" Viktoria added in a matter of fact tone.

"I will stay until we find your mother or father; I have to get back to my hotel and it is a way tonight". Brandon answered dryly with an added sense of calm.

"Let's go inside" Viktoria replied with a higher pitch to her voice, Brandon understood she must not have felt safe; she has been a bit scared and just wanted him to find her parents.

Brandon walked with Viktoria to the doorway of the manor. There were no lights and it grew colder, due to the wind rushing against the manor. Viktoria held out her left hand and opened the door.

The manor looked as if it had not been painted for years; the dilapidated house, despite its appearance, had a very heavy door. Upon opening the door, a smell of what can be described as "old" and "decay" crept out from the doorway. The entryway was very oppressive; the somewhat wide staircase was old, yet fully intact. The floor itself was what appeared to once have been black and white checkered tiles, yet the white, either due to the twilight or dirt, was a dark gray.

The stairs, off to the right once they walked through the door, one flight up to a rest area with a dark stained window, then another flight going up into a darker area he could not see. Before he could notice, the door which they both entered through closed. Brandon was not sure if he or Viktoria had closed it.

"Please come in, Mommie is here somewhere." Viktoria said.

The door ahead of them was dirt-stained dark yellow, with no elaborate carvings or designs. It was opened and darkness was within the next room. Walking forward, Brandon realized Viktoria was nearly out of sight just ahead of him.

The book felt heavy now, well, *heavier* than before.

Listening to the sounds coming from the next room, Brandon could make out a voice, an old woman's voice, raspy and cold sounding. She spoke in what sounded to be labored breaths in the Romanian language. While Brandon did not recognize what she actually said, he did get the abrupt, nearly machine-gun attack of the voice.

Brandon stopped in his tracks; he just felt awkward here, thinking to himself "How will I explain this? The woman must be a grandmother, she will not understand that I was tripping with Viktoria's mother's and father's occult gathering…"

For a moment more, he slowly licked his bottom lip as a reflex of nervousness.

He felt so nervous as a matter of fact that insects seemed to be moving under his skin, his scalp was warm and tingly, a sure sign of the feeling of complete anxiety.

Brandon Kestle understood that he would just turn around and walk out of the room, moving out of sight and hopefully out of mind in due course. "I have just had enough of all this".

Before turning around, Viktoria chimed "Please come…here", her English not so clear at the moment. The voice drew closer and Brandon at the last second decided to just go in the room.

"How the fuck will I explain this?" he thought frantically while looking at the near dark yellow-white walls with cobwebs and a bit of dirt at the base of the wall and floor.

"I can tell this woman that I came back to the place where I was with the parents last night; I saw Viktoria and I wanted to get her home. I have not seen her parents since last evening, from which I left earlier…" Calm began to enter; his arms, neck and legs felt the warmth of peaceful thoughts for that second.

Another plus, his sight was getting better in the dark here; these moments of panic can really bring some things to the forefront.

Brandon, with the large book at his side, just walked forward, which opened up into a larger drawing area. The only light in this room was a candelabrum near the window some 20 feet away, near a window which is covered in large green drapery. There were pictures and paintings on the wall and from what he could first glance, they were obviously old, but that was all he could tell at the moment. Anxiety was creeping back.

Walking in he could see in the near dark a chair with an old woman sitting in it, dressed in what *appeared* to be either black or dark brown with a scarf over her head. She was dangling Viktoria's doll over the arm of the large parlor chair. Adjacent to him, he noticed a mirror on the wall. A dark frame around it was carved nicely, from what he could tell.

The room smelled ripe, almost like meat that had sat out a bit long, wasn't yet *quite* bad but could get there if it sat too much longer. The ceilings were so high it was actually refreshing to be in here. Brandon glanced at different sections of the ceiling, which had some type of decoration in certain random areas!

"How odd..." he thought, wondering why in the hell they would decorate the ceiling.

Viktoria walked behind him with soft steps, only her dull black dress shoes making slight clicks on the floor. Brandon heard other steps with her, like other softer legs...this had to be the ambiance of the room causing that sound.

Brandon turned around to greet Viktoria; he glanced at her face, slightly over-shadowed by him standing in the specific light reflection of the candelabra at the opposite end of the room.

Viktoria seemed so pale, with a greenish light dancing off the side of her face. It was as if for this instance, everything went slower, like time was not counting here...

"Hello there", Brandon said, turning to the direction of the grandmother in the chair. He practically ignored Viktoria to make his case with the old woman, who he still could not see clearly.

"I am Brandon Kes..." he could not finish his sentence before he heard the howling in the room, surrounding him, causing him to shake at the frequency of the howling and chattering from all sides.

"AZ-A-THOTH BECOMES, GATE OPENED!" - a voice from behind him.

Brandon turned to face a sight which caused his pallor to become dead-white, his blood felt so cold and that nagging-nervous feeling of insects under his skin came back.

Viktoria stood out of his shadow to reveal her obviously mutating body. Her eyes were black without any white *at all*.

Veins in her face where black-blue and spider-like, her mouth opened and black blood seeped out as she spoke in a voice only partially her own. The other voice he heard was the one he heard in what he recalled as the nightmare.

"Come now, Legion, AZATHOTH COMMANDS IT" it sputtered, insect legs tearing her clothes and touching the floor, taking the main body-weight as it lifted her up from the ground.

Brandon felt the pains of nausea and turned in shock.

The grandmother stood up and came closer to him in a posture which was not much like an elderly person. Her legs were shown bare from a tear in the robe she was wearing, it looked so old! Her toes, which he could see, were like talons, animal-like and covered in what looked like some dark blood-like substance.

She lifted the doll up with her right arm, and as she did this, her other spider-thin hand took hold of it by the neck and brought it up to her mouth. The hag opened her dark mouth and bit deep into the dolls neck area.

The only thing was that it was not a doll….and it was already dead!

Brandon could see her top few teeth and they were like razors…as she bit down, the fangs disappeared like the sun vanishing to bring darkness; the empty pale white eyes of the child did not flinch but the mouth opened like it was attempting to cry out.

A great stench filled the room; looking down, the floor felt as if it was moving yet it was insects below. Brandon's sense of panic nearly overtook him.

"Why…what the fuck!" The possessed atmosphere seemed so real, yet almost like an illusion. As soon as this thought was finished, he felt a cold hand touch his…Viktoria or the thing which took her body as its covering, and all instance of wondering whether or not it was real was confirmed.

The hag hissed at him in a language he did not understand for an instance, it was similar to what was chanted at the old warehouse during the malevolent rites. She turned back to look at the chair, moved quickly over to it and reached down with a guttural chant.

With the small undead child gripped tightly by her left hand, she now reached down and picked up something which had a moist sticky sound as it was lifted up. What Brandon could see at this moment was what she was actually sitting on.

The main cushion of the seat had been removed and there was a pile of heads from the floor up. The hag was making a chair of human heads!

The head she held up looked as if it had been half eaten, or much of the face and muscle removed. The hag looked at it briefly, then looking back to Brandon, the hag tossed it almost gently towards him, as if it was a child and an adult playing toss in the backyard or at a family gathering. Avoiding it, the thud it made while hitting the floor made him nearly shiver. The mouth was moving, like a near-biting motion from a head already half-eaten!

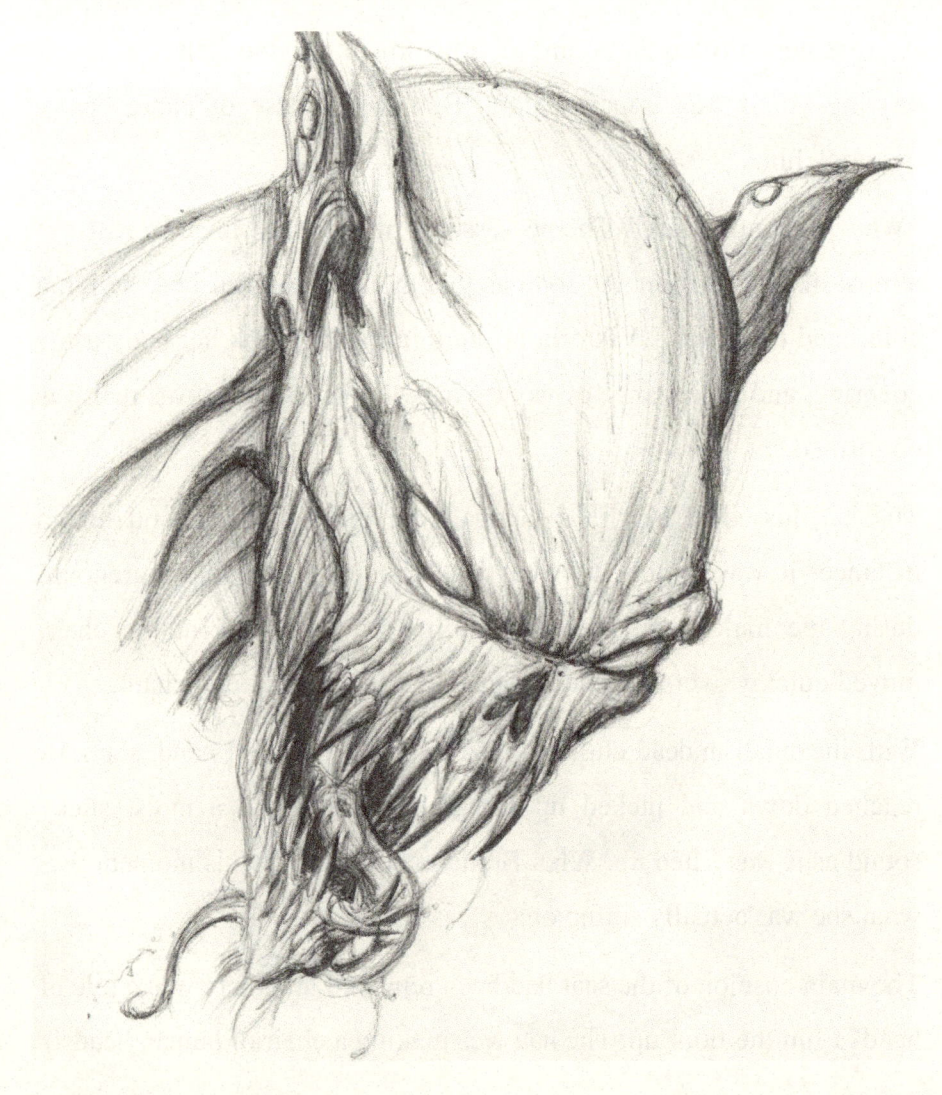

Looking back at the heads, Brandon could now see that they were all moving, the heads were actually biting each other! This disgusting sight was too much to ponder, he just wanted to leave and get away.

Brandon dropped the book and started to turn. He caught his reflection in the mirror.

He could not believe it, how could this be?

Covered in blood, Brandon's face was ghost-pale and with a pinkish hue under his eyes. His lips were almost blue and those same spider veins in Viktoria's face were now in his! He felt his body being pushed outward in several spots, like the dream he had the night before meeting this abomination of a cult. Looking down, his clothes were covered in what appeared to be old blood, how could he not have seen this?

"We have been waiting child, you have tried to delay this but you cannot stop what is your past." An obviously broken neck with what was Viktoria's head spoke with small swarms of flies coming from her mouth as she uttered these words, sounding like an old woman and a sick child at the same time.

"You already belong to us, now give us your flesh – and soul" a high pitched whisper came from near his right ear which moved away in a flash when Brandon slightly turned towards it.

"Ecstasy awaits…" came a cracking, long dead-sounding voice from the corner. Its accent was nearly absent, insinuating that it could have been merely an echo in his head or worse - the demonic shapes could be speaking only to him.

Is this madness, no it is worse?!

"Speak its name, speak its name!" came a voice from above him.

Looking up while feeling the surge of what felt like insects under his skin, Brandon glanced at the shadow figure above him, which resembled some strange piece of art that was part of the darkness which enveloped the room.

Its stature was difficult to estimate, although it must have been nearly six feet tall. The body itself was a blood clotted hue with deathly white patches under the skin. Its eyes were black as night and the mouth of this thing was closed. The hair was missing in patches and it was only wearing what appeared to be shredded dress slacks. The demon-infested body was twisted in an odd manner, hands and feet twisted behind to hold itself to the ceiling.

The right hand left its place from the ceiling, the forefinger now pointing down at Brandon in a motion that took a millisecond.

The mouth opened to spit forth a black bile and an otherworldly scream deep from its throat.

Suddenly before him, a shape emerged from the floor as a black shadow, gathering mass as it arose as a blackened pit from the now engulfed floor below it. The shape took the form of a cloaked figure, slightly taller than Brandon.

He could not see within this blackened mass before him. The room's energy changed even more, hearing the howling of things all around him, his own body changing and moving beneath his skin. The atmosphere felt as if everything had moved upward into a mountain. It seemed as if the energy was being drawn into this blackened shadow.

Making a guttural, and at the same time whispering sound, the shadow-mass before him emanated the sounds of insects and hungering, rabid animals. Hearing the flapping of wings from it, many crow-like shadows emerged from it, encircling Brandon in flight.

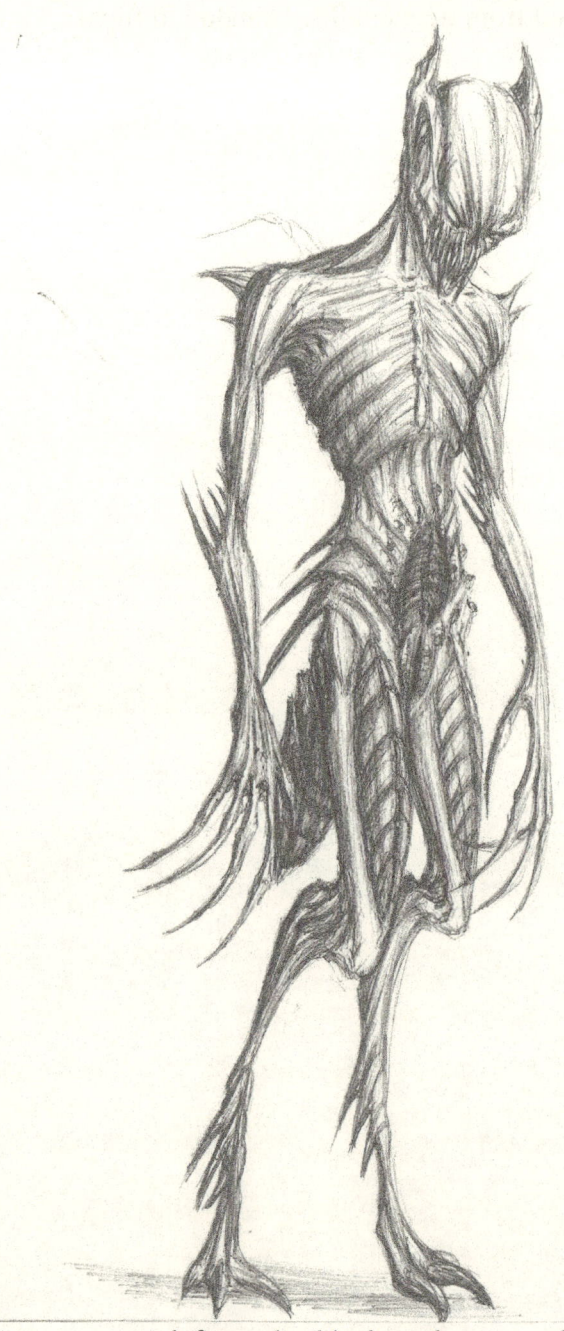

Arms emerged from the blackened mass, which were also complete pitch black. The only two things which could be discerned were that the fingers were long and spider-thin and that there was also a robe-like sleeve covering its arm, being drawn back by the arms and hands extending nearly upward.

The face, which could now be seen as it formed features, looked bone thin, eyes which were a deep burning red like they were reflected against any remaining light in the room. Brandon could discern a nose which extended down as if the thing before him was of Middle Eastern descent, large lips extended to show billowing insects emerging from the darkness.

The piercing cry was like a sharp howl and sounded as if it amplified the cries of numerous victims who were having their skin peeled off.

Brandon felt as if he could not go on any longer; he looked into the eyes of the blackened shape. To his right side now came Viktoria, or the thing which wore her shell of a body, now damaged and blackened with blood.

As Brandon glared into the eyes of the daemon-sultan, who took the form he wished in this world, his sense of time vanished.

"Welcome my child, you should feel pride that you were chosen. It is time to be our gateway, come to your father. Soon it will be born; soon it will ride the nightmares of so many more than the desert wastelands of sometime past."

Brandon ignored everything around him and walked towards the one called Azathoth. As he walked into the otherworldly shape, he understood at once.

"My dreams shape the world you walk in, your blood and this race from which you ascend from give us physical being. We shall dwell in it together. Let the gates open now!"

"We travel by nightmare and you will strengthen us! The seven are one, the unnamable one will rise!"

A great sound engulfed the house, a howling rushed through as the barrier seemed to expand and then close again.

In a flash there was silence.

There was complete darkness…

SIGIL OF AZATHOTH

AFTERWORD

The old manor only seemed empty.

In the room where the shadows took flesh, there were nine Individuals. They sat where they could, some on the floor, some in chairs. An old lady normally sat in the chair where the heads were stacked before, yet no heads could be seen.

Brandon sat upright in a seeming Yoga position as he looked forward at the old woman. His hair was kept and he was clean. His jacket had no blood and next to him, now on the left, was little Viktoria. Her dress was fresh and she had a mischievous smile on her face.

Everything was normal, except they were not moving and the room was pitch black.

Brandon's eyes shifted, they were that deep blood red as the Azathoth shape which embraced him. With a blink, his eyes were again his normal color of hazel.

It was time to get up; there was much to do in this world.

They were all very hungry and they have waited long enough.

END

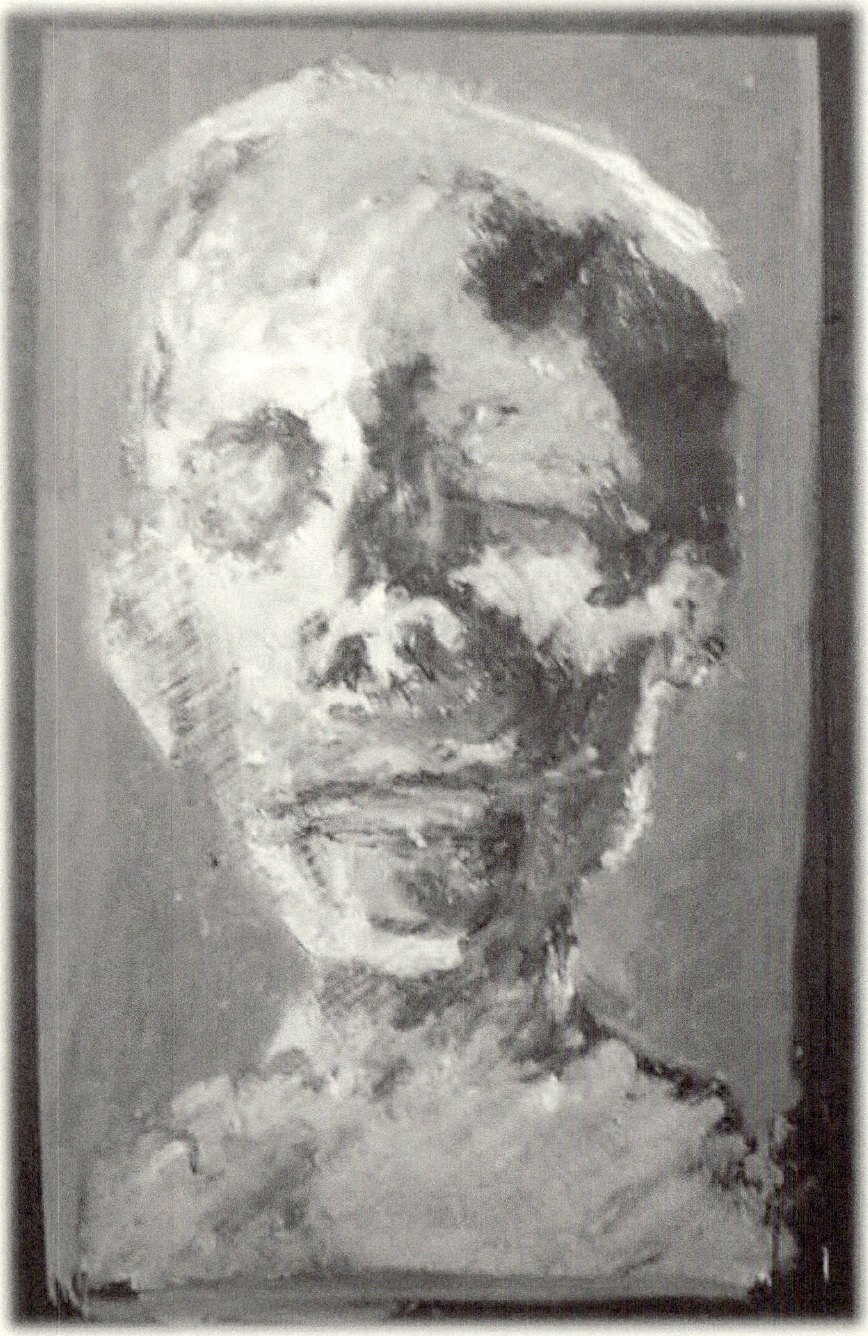

THE HUNGERING ONE

BY MICHAEL W. FORD

ONE: SICKNESS AND THE LEGS OF INSECTS

The life of a Temple Prostitute can be a very difficult life, if you are not of the upper class that is able to serve Ishtar in her place of worship. The young woman who lays sick with fever on the dirt floor, whose diseased body is host to something which is bringing her to death, was a "curse" from the Gods from what her father believes. His labor as a plowman does little to lift them from squalor.

For two days the young girl, once very pretty and from her few short years as a prostitute, servicing the squalor of this Chaldean city has really brought a toll on her both inside and out. Her skin, dark and youthful has turned a yellowish-gray with her sweating sickness. Consciousness fades in and out as the taste of dust saturates her mouth. She falls asleep in the burning rays of the sun upon their hut, being drawn to dreams which cannot be remembered.

The young woman's eyes open, a thin crust formed at the edges causes her to slowly and clumsily wipe it away. She feels weaker than ever, sweating profusely she tries to move yet is unable. Each attempt at movement is increasingly painful. While it seems there is no moon out tonight, there is also little breeze and it remains very stuffy.

Not being able to move, the sick woman looks around her fathers' small hut. Normally the eyes adapt well to the night and all areas can be seen to some extent, yet the corner near her left side was filled with blackness, like a great enveloping mist of consuming darkness embodied it. Her father slept over in front of her, he gave no movement, even with her intentional whimpering.

For so long in her temple duties she had prayed for something to come and guide her away from all this, tirelessly laying in submission for men to finish inside of her, countless herbs which cause horrid sickness to abort unwanted fetuses until she contracted some disease. This cursed disease brought her to the point she is now, laying in partial death, waiting for her body to collapse further.

The young prostitutes' mind went back to the gathering and foreboding darkness in the corner. She noticed something moving in the darkness, like waves of the ocean which were against the area. Towards the hut covering above them, something like a giant spider slowly crawled from the mass, before she could notice below; the mass was flowing into this insect-demon which was the size of a man.

An intense fear gripped her and before she could take another breath the demon leaped from the hut roof inside and spun around to the dirt floor below, rushing towards her in the semi-form of a man. Expanding wings, what appeared to be black feathers had talon-like hooks from the top of them, while the legs of the demon were like a lion, yet terminating into bird-like claws perching it ever-so slightly into the dirt floor.

The demon stood taller than a normal man, it's body covered in what looked like scales and a lion like skull which was covered in tight pale-gray skin, a nose which was hooked and eyes which burned crimson with black circles.

Before she could cry out a black-clawed hand covered her mouth in with lightening speed and with a grip so tight she could not even move her body.

"You have been seized by Labsu, who rested in the body of the man you lay with. You will die in deep sickness and it will be more painful than this…" whispered the demon in the tongue of her people, the language ringing out in her mind when it looked into her eyes.

"Screaming would only cause your fathers' death, do you wish to see me tear his throat and feast upon his life?" it muttered…

"Of course not…I will take my hand away and you will not scream or cry out." The demon commanded.

Feeling the pull to obey this command, the sick woman did not scream.

"I give you now a choice, die here and without any possibility of survival, to be food for the Gods or accept my sacrament and live on to be a daughter of our great Mother."

"If you choose to stay here I will rip you apart anyway, to satisfy my cravings." The demon spoke clearly into her mind…the girl knew she had one option.

"I accept, I am so tired…" the sick woman surrendered.

The head of the demon slightly shifted, as if it were studying her with the emotion of an insect.

With a flick of the long, cruel black talon of the right index finger, the demon cut into the left wrist which was covered in what appeared to be scales and dark brown hair or fur. Its mouth was agape and a forked tongue darted out like a serpent smelling its environment. The face of the demon shifted in an instant to a man, pale with death that had little human features.

The wrist was then placed to her mouth with a strength which could not be considered by a normal man. She could not move and as quick as her hands gripped his arm she was soon holding it in place to drink.

The black blood was thick and held a sweet and soon intense emotion. She drank and felt her strength returning in these moments. Bliss overtook her and she felt moist between her legs. Drinking, she felt the black liquid fill her mouth and slowly fill her throat. Emotions of hunger, of power and feeding from others consumed her. In this moment she was thrilled she had chosen this path, which this demon had chosen her as well.

In the next instant the now enraptured prostitute felt the blood begin to spring up what felt like insects from the blood, which filled her mouth and crawled down her throat. Panic overcame her, terror replaced ecstasy and she felt as if she was drowning. The demon pressed harder as its face shape shifted back into the lion-skull which it bore. The upper body pulsated with insects and the outline of serpents under the black and gray skin, spitting, she choked on the bile so a small amount dribbled down the corner of her mouth to her ear.

Releasing she inhaled with a ferocity which should have collapsed her lungs, coughing and then spitting black blood and scattering, crawling insects upon her now bear chest and cloth covering her genitals.

The demon, now squatted from offering her blood, opened its mouth wide and revealed razor sharp teeth. The fangs were so numerous she could not believe it and the mouth of the demon extended and cracked as if it was shape changing. The nose of the demon curled up as a vampire-bat and large ears grew from the side of the skull. In an instant, he gurgled a howling like sound and with a falling force slammed its head into her right side of the throat, ignoring the sweat-caked hair seemingly stuck to it.

She felt pressure and a stinging sensation, the head of the demon vibrating back and forth causing her to grow weak from blood loss. In a few moments she heard her father scream and shout calling the demon to leave, before she lost consciousness she felt a violent release and the demon in a surreal movement went sideways in a composite form of a bat and black bird out the hut window.

Passing out, she drifted to nightmares, her father screaming and howling in fear and sobbing tears.

The prostitute had now been kissed to enter the cult of Ardat Lili by Idlu Lili, the male demon-vampire of the night. Her "life" or "undeath" is just to begin.

The hours of the day were spent in heat and a plethora of flies. The father could not work this day as he had to bury his daughter, the only offspring he had. Mother had died from sickness some years before. With a grave dug under where she would normally sleep, father had gently placed his child into the ground. There were no priests to come and chant over her, to protect her from the night. He could only hope she found rest from the horrific event of the previous evening.

Her face had been cleaned as much as he could, she smelled of rot and sickness still. Covering her in a cloth – wrapping, he face was left unconcealed. He prayed to the Gods and covered her. The sun was setting as he placed her favorite items – a small bracelet from her mother and some small idols at the head of her burial place. Father grew tired and ate very little. He then offered drink in to the Gods.

Night came with somber mood; father fell to sleep in emptiness. He would wake in the morning and go to work to be screamed at for missing several days; even with his daughters' sickness and death.

TWO: NIGHT AND REBIRTH

Consciousness emerged to a voice which a night before was in her head. The nightmare was now a waking dream. The young woman tried to open her eyes however could take no breath. Feeling strong, the woman tore through the earth until her hands were free in the air. With a violent jerk she rose up from the shallow grave her father prepared. At the moment she rose up and inhaled deeply, it was so good to breathe air again. Everything looked different however, she could see extremely well in the night. Her small hut she had grown up in, been molested in by her father and sold into prostitution after her mothers' death really felt like a different person, she felt brand new.

In front of her, the demon who had attacked her the night previously now appeared as a black robed man, although very pale with the same burning eyes and sharp, black talons on extended skeletal fingers. His feet were still those of a bird of prey however not very noticeable with the long black goatskin robe.

"Good evening my sister, I knew you would awaken and feel different about things…I am no longer your enemy but your savior." He said bluntly.

"Yes…hungry…very thirsty." The young woman said. She felt her skin tightening. Looking at her hands, she noticed the nails had turned black and extended nearly four inches to razor sharp talons. She had bluish-gray veins under her skin. Her tongue touched her upper teeth and she felt two very sharp extended as she noticed her hunger.

"You will be able to control your flesh my sister, my mother and other family will teach you the way however first you must feed" said the Idlu Lili.

Looking over to her sleeping father, the new Ardat Lili, the former prostitute looked away and answered "NO!"

"Who molested your flesh, sold you into being a less than sacred whore and finally – who killed your mother?" asked the demon.

"My mother was sick…" she answered firmly.

"Your mother was poisoned by your father…" the Idlu Lili answered quickly.

"I don't believe you…" she quickly responded.

"Ask her yourself"…the demon then uttered a prayer calling the Ekimmu and a great wind surrounded the hut. Her father sprang upward wiping his eyes as if hallucinating.

"What…is this?" her father mumbled in disbelief.

He was not asking his newly risen-from-the-dead daughter, still shrouded in a caked dirt and dried blood cloth, a face as pale and spider-veined with the very mask of the demoness of night. Nor was he asking to the Idlu Lili, the male demon who stood beside her.

He asked this to the shape of a long worn shade, uttering something over and over again.

At this moment the newly arisen vampire knew that her mother was murdered, her shade was here to torment the man she called father.

"Feed now and without regret, for the Ekimmu will take care of the rest" said the Idlu Lili.

Her arms reaching out, a great screech let out from her mouth and the newly awakened Ardat Lili lunged at her father. She bit into his face with razor teeth, getting a small taste of blood. She thrashed at his body, cutting into him so fast he could not scream nor stop it. Finally her teeth found his throat and she bit as deep as she could. Warm, fresh blood filled her mouth and she greedily drank all she could. Falling back he was slowly dying and she loved every moment of it.

Feeling full and calmer, she noticed he was dead. Standing up quickly the shade of her mother, who did not recognize her hovered over to him, wind tearing through the hut.

"Let us go my sister, we shall teach you the ways" said the male demon. The young woman nodded her head and felt only happiness for her future. "This is what it is like to be a Goddess" she thought.

With one arm he covered her and they turned into a cloud of black wind, hissing and howling in the night as they went forth towards the desert wilderness. The neighbors had heard the howling winds and muffled cries however did not dare move to see what it was. Only death awaited the curious.

Above the city that night were the cries of black birds and owls…the dwellers of the city knew they were waiting for them.

CULT OF THE WAR-GOD

The Hidden Vampiric Cult of Tiamat

BY MICHAEL W. FORD

I DARK ABYSSIC ORIGINS

Ashurnasirpal II (883 – 859 BC) was an Assyrian King whose aggressive policy of subduing the neighbors (in the ancient near east, 'neighbors' would often be identical with the word 'enemy') not only saved the Assyrian Kingdom; it caused it to flourish.

Yet as within the world since the beginning of human history, being often in harmony with nature we destroy and create.

The ancient pantheons of the Near East are filled with Gods and Goddesses, Demons and Spirits of the Dead who are often balanced. Like humans they possess moods, characters and the Gods express their wide range of emotions via Nature: that by which the God is attributed to. The conquering gods rule over the consistency of nature, the world and those who build and maintain the Temple Cults. This is by which the world works; the strong conquer the weak and the clever dominate the strong; just as in the natural world of animals, plants and all forms of living organisms.

Often forgotten in our origins is that from which we emerged from: the dark abyssic waters of chaos.

Tiamat, known also as Omoroca and Thalatth is the representation of the ancient salt water sea. Tiamat could assume many forms and after finding her offspring rebelling against her nightmarish darkness and dreaming sleep, she assumed a terrible serpent-dragon form and created a great army of chaos-monsters to battle the usurping gods. She clothed them in the terrifying radiance or 'melammu'. The husband of Tiamat was Kingu, the inventor of war who commanded her army as General. Marduk and the gods fought against chaos and soon won this great battle. Tiamat's dragon-form was used to shape the world and Kingu's blood was used to create humanity.

The gods' established a great order and many chaos-monsters and demons joined the balance of the Marduk, Ea, Enlil and the rest. The gods blended with aspects of nature and were fed by the offerings of the Temple Cults. What the gods did not know was that Tiamat could not die; she was their origin and was not mortal. Her consciousness was so great she compelled the fate (she created the Tablet of Destinies) of the gods to create her next manifestation through the evolution of nature. Only her 'form' was destroyed, she simply remanifested in a spiritual sense as the goddess Ishtar.

Marduk consumed a libation bowl full of the blood of Kingu before man was made, as also did Ea and the storm god Enlil which made them very powerful. Kingu was also an immortal chaos-demon; while his physical form was destroyed his psyche remained. Kingu could silently assume the consciousness of the gods without their knowledge. The demons of outer darkness had a gateway in which they could enter our world, when opportunity presented itself the powers of darkness could compel humans through their blood to make offerings to not only the gods (Ishtar, Marduk) yet all the while offering to Tiamat and Kingu.

Tiamat could compel great power to her worshippers; we see that from the records of Sargon I, Naram-Sin and here Ashurnasirpal II; Assur the Assyrian god (Marduk) is worshipped in a public sense as his conquering glory, yet in the secret cult temple records found only recently we find instead the great conquests and mass-killings of enemies were performed as libations to Tiamat and Kingu. Ashurnasirpal II entered the cult to gain power; he found that as Ishtar (Tiamat hidden within) and Assur (Kingu hidden within) that the blood offerings could be used to temporarily open 'abyssic gateways' into the astral realm of the primordial chaos – and those who dream within it. A human-skull bowl was made as a libation holder; Ashurnasirpal in the hidden cults of the night would physically pass a libation of blood through and in turn it was filled with a type of black blood. Ashurnasirpal drank this libation and over a period of one moon cycle was transformed into a vampiric being.

Forget the legends; Ashurnasirpal found his form could assume various monster and animal shapes; a gift from the Blood of Tiamat, yet during the daylight and campaigns he would maintain a perfectly healthy human form. His thirst for blood and war grew and his great killings and offerings were kept to the enemies of Assyria. If he did not have continual war his desire would turn on his own people; thus fortunately for the King Assyria required stability and direct confrontation through conquering.

The following is from unearthed tablets found in the ruins of Kalhu (the biblical Calah of Genesis 10:12) or as it is known today, Nimrud. While some aspects of these records are identical to the known 'official' records, modern scholars have determined that this particular tablet (found in what was a temple to a large 'Musmah' serpent-dragon which is identified as Tiamat) is what now appears to be part record/part incantation text to opening the gates of the underworld.

II MUSHUSSU UNLEASHED
The Discovered Secret Cult Records of Ashurnasirpal II

The translated tablets found in the ruins of Kalhu:
"Ashurnasirpal, attentive prince, worshipper of the great gods, ferocious dragon (Mushussu), conqueror of cities and the entire highlands, king of lords, encircler of the obstinate, crowned with splendor (Melammu), fearless in battle, merciless hero, he who stirs up strife, praiseworthy king, shepherd, protection of the (four) quarters, the king whose command disintegrates mountains and seas, the one who by his lordly conflict has brought under one authority ferocious and merciless kings from east to west:

I have traversed mighty mountains; I have seen remote and rugged regions throughout all the (four) quarters; I have caused flaming arrows to rain down upon the princes of all cities (so that) they ever revere my command and pray to my lordship; in one region my army set up camp, gathering several slaves I went forth with guard and the Priests of Assur. In oracle it was Assur which offered me the Kingship and rule over the world; Ishtar of Nineveh would be my mistress into this path of the dragon.

In a mountain cave my priests led me to a place wherein they offered the blood of the slaves who were flayed alive and beheaded. This offering was placed within a deep pool of blackened blood which was opened to us from Enlil and Ishtar of Nineveh.

It was here that the mysteries would be opened for me; that I would bring the world under my domination for the glory of Ishtar, Assur and the gods above and below. I, Ashurnasirpal, sage, expert, intelligent one, open to counsel and wisdom which the god Ea, king of the *absu*, destined for me; the great gods of heaven and underworld chose me, in their steadfast hearts, and my sovereignty, dominion, and power came forth by their command; they sternly commanded me to rule, subdue, and direct the lands and mighty highlands: Ashurnasirpal, strong king, king of Assyria, designate of the god Sîn, favourite of the god Anu, loved one of the god Adad who is almighty among the gods, I, the merciless weapon which lays low lands hostile to him, for I alone am instructed by the divine essence of Kingu, the chosen King of Tiamat.

I, the king, capable in battle, vanquisher of cities and highlands, foremost in battle, king of the four quarters, the one who defeats his enemies, the king who disintegrates all his enemies, king of the totality of the four quarters including all their princes, the king who forces to bow down those insubmissive to him, the one who rules all peoples; these destinies came forth at the command of the great gods and they properly fixed them as my destinies.

FLAYING OF THE RULER OF NISTUN AND THE PILE OF HEADS

Because of my voluntary offerings and my prayers the goddess Istar (Tiamat), the mistress who loves my priesthood, approved of me and she made up her mind to make war and battle, Moving on from Mount Kirruru I entered the pass which (leads from) the city Hulun to the interior of the land Habhu. I conquered the cities Hattu, Hataru, Nistun, Sabidi, Metqia, Arsania, Tela, Halua, cities of the land Habhu which lie between Mounts Usu, Arua, & Arardi, mighty mountains.

I massacred many of them and carried off prisoners and possessions from them. The troops were frightened and took to a lofty peak in front of the city Nistun, which hovered like a cloud in the sky. Into the midst of those which none of the kings my fathers had ever approached my warriors flew like birds. I felled 260 of their combat troops with the sword. I cut off their heads and formed (therewith) a pile. The rest of them built nests like birds on mountain precipices. I brought down prisoners and possessions of theirs from the mountain and I razed, destroyed, and burnt the cities which lay within the mighty highlands.

The troops, as many as had fled from my weapons, came down and submitted to me. I imposed upon them tribute and tax. Būbu, son of Babua, son of the city ruler of the city Ništun, I flayed in the city Arbail and draped his skin over the wall. At that time I made an image of myself and wrote thereon the praises of my power. I erected (it) on the mountain in the city (called) Ashurnasirpal at the source of the spring.

CITY OF KINABU AND THE PILE OF CORPSES

I crossed over to Mount Kasiiari and approached the city Kinabu, the fortified city of Hulāiia. With the mass of my troops and my fierce battle I besieged and conquered the city. I felled with the sword 800 of their combat troops, I burnt 3,000 captives from them. I did not leave one of them alive as a hostage. I captured alive Hulāiia their city ruler. I made a pile of their corpses. I burnt their adolescent boys and girls; I flayed Hulaiia their city ruler and draped his skin over the wall of the city Damdammusa. I razed, destroyed, and burnt the city. I conquered the city Mariru which was in their environs.

I felled 50 of their fighting-men with the sword, burnt 200 captives from them, and defeated in a battle on the plain 332 troops of the land Nirbu. I brought back prisoners, oxen, (and) sheep from them. The (inhabitants of) the land Nirbu, which is at the foot of Mount Uhira, banded together and entered the city Tela, their fortified city.

Moving on from the city Kinabu I approached the city Tela. The city was well fortified; it was surrounded by three walls. The people put their trust in their strong walls and their large number of troops and did not come down to me.

They did not submit to me.

In strife and conflict I besieged and conquered the city. I felled 3,000 of their fighting men with the sword. I carried off prisoners, possessions, oxen, and cattle from them. I burnt many captives from them. I captured many troops alive: from some I cut off their arms and hands; from others I cut off their noses, ears, and *extremities.*

I gouged out the eyes of many troops. I made one pile of the living and one of heads. I hung their heads on trees around the city; I burnt their adolescent boys and girls. I razed, destroyed, burnt, and consumed the city. At that time I razed, destroyed, and burnt the cities of the land Nirbu and their strong walls.

CONSUMING THE CITY OF TELA: THE SEVERED HEADS UPON TREES

Moving on from the city Kinabu I approached the city Tela. The city was well fortified; it was surrounded by three walls. The people put their trust in their strong walls and their large number of troops and did not come down to me. They did not submit to me. In strife and conflict I besieged and conquered the city. I felled 3,000 of their fighting men with the sword. I carried off prisoners, possessions, oxen, and cattle from them. I burnt many captives from them. I captured many troops alive: from some I cut off their arms and hands; from others I cut off their noses, ears, and *extremities.*

I gouged out the eyes of many troops. I made one pile of the living and one of heads. I hung their heads on trees around the city; I burnt their adolescent boys and girls. I razed, destroyed, burnt, and consumed the city. At that time I razed, destroyed, and burnt the cities of the land Nirbu and their strong walls.

THE BLOOD COVERED MOUNTAIN AND OFFERING TO AZAG

On my return from the lands Nairi, the land Nirbu which is within Mount Kasiiari rebelled. They abandoned their nine cities (and) trusted in the city Išpiiipria, their fortified city, and a rugged mountain. But I besieged and conquered the mountain peaks. Within the mighty mountain I massacred them. With their blood I dyed the mountain red like red wool and the rest of them the ravines and torrents of the mountain swallowed. I carried off captives and possessions from them. I cut off the heads of their fighters and built (therewith) a tower before their city. I burnt their adolescent boys (and) girls.

Moving on from this camp I marched to the cities in the plain of Mount Nisir which no one had ever seen. I conquered the city Larbusa, the fortified city which (was ruled by) Kirteara, and eight cities in its environs. The troops were frightened and took to a rugged mountain. The mountain was as jagged as the point of a dagger.

The king with his troops climbed up after them. I threw down their corpses in the mountain, massacred 172 of their fighting men, and piled up many troops on the precipices of the mountain. I brought back captives, possessions, oxen, (and) sheep from them and burnt their cities. I hung their heads on trees of the mountain and burnt their adolescent boys and girls. I returned to my camp and spent the night. I offered many prisoners and their blood to Azag, the great demon of the Mountains; the Priests of Tiamat and Kingu offered up the Tablets of Destiny which I offered blood upon in the name of our mother, Tiamat, who wore the form of Ishtar.

I conquered the city Kūkunu which is at the entrance to the pass of Mount Matnu. I felled with the sword 700 of their fighting-men. I carried off many captives from them. I conquered 50 cities of the Dirru. I massacred them, carried off prisoners from them, and captured 50 soldiers alive. I razed, destroyed, and burnt the cities. I unleashed against them my lordly radiance, Moving on from the city Pitura I went down to the city Arbakku in the interior of the land

Habhu. They took fright in the face of my royal radiance and abandoned their cities and walls. To save their lives they climbed up Mount Matnu, a mighty mountain. I went after them. I slew 1,000 of their men-at-arms within the rugged mountain, dyed the mountain red with their blood, and filled the ravines and torrents of the mountain with their corpses. I captured 200 soldiers alive and cut off their arms. I carried off 2,000 captives from them. I brought back oxen and sheep from them without number. I conquered the cities Iiaia (and) Salaniba, fortified cities of the city Arbakku. I massacred and carried off prisoners from them. I razed, destroyed, and turned into ruin hills 250 of their well-fortified cities of the lands Nairi.

THE FORTIFIED CITY OF KAPRABU AND BLOOD TO KINGU

On the twentieth day of the month Sivan I moved from Calah. After crossing **the** Tigris I marched to the land Bit-Adini and approached the city Kaprabu, their fortified city. The city was well fortified; it hovered like a cloud in the sky. The people, trusting in their numerous troops, did not come down and submit to me.

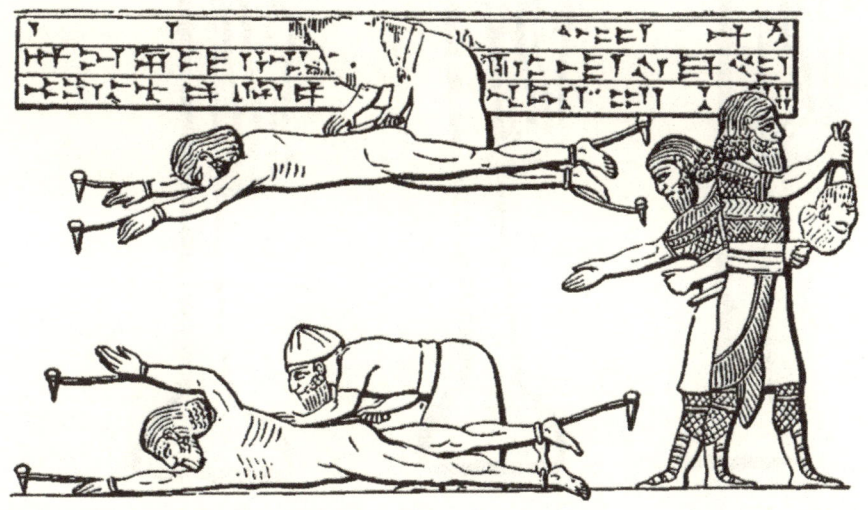

By the command of Kingu, who manifested as Aššur, the great lord, my lord, and **the** divine standard which goes before me, I besieged the city and conquered it by means of tunnels, battering-rams, and siege towers. I massacred many of them; I slew 800 of their men-at-arms, and carried off captives (and) property from them. I uprooted 2,500 of their troops and settled them in Calah. I razed, destroyed, burnt, and consumed the city. (Thus) I imposed awe of the radiance of Aššur, my lord, upon Blt-Adini.

IMPALED SOLDIERS AROUND THE CITY OF LABTURU

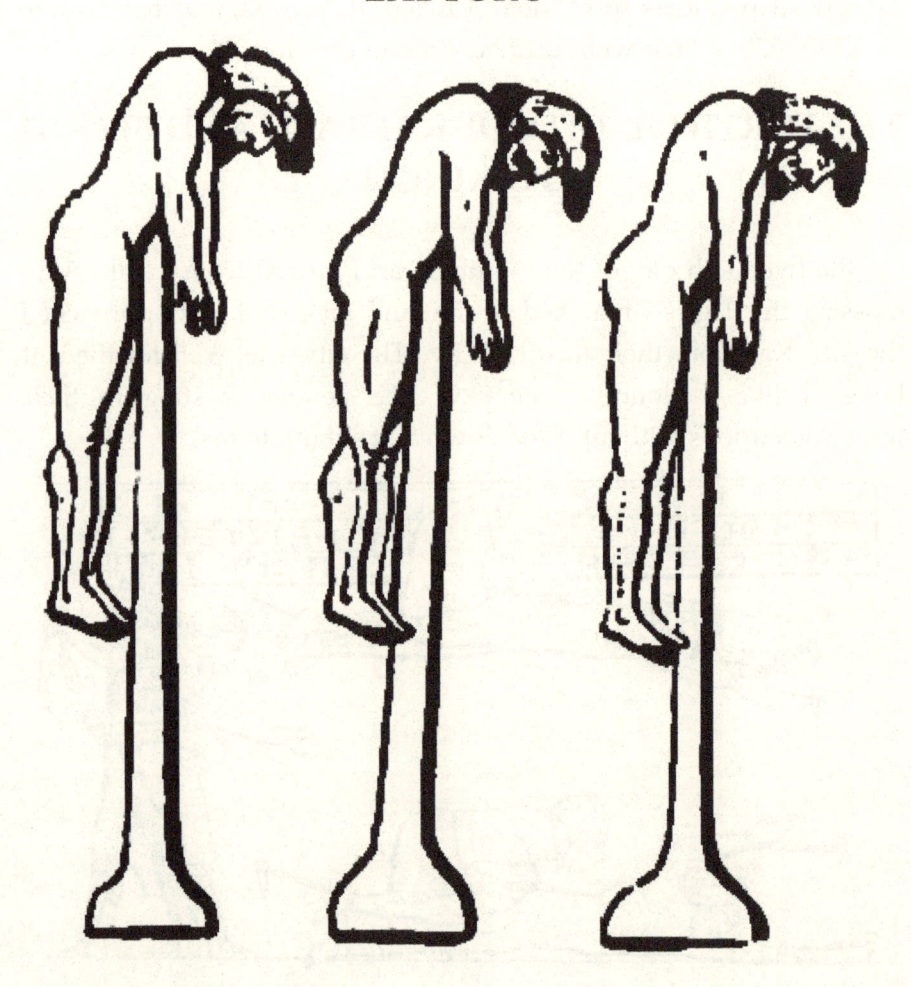

Moving on from the land Maliānu I burnt the cities of the land Zamba which were in the region of my path. After crossing the River Sua I pitched camp by the Tigris. I turned into ruin hills the cities which lie on this bank and the other bank of the Tigris at Mount Arkania. All of the land Habhu took fright and submitted to me. I took hostages from them and appointed a governor of my own over them. I came out of the pass of Mount Amadānu to the city Barzaništun. I approached the city Damdammusa, the fortified city of Ilānu, a man of Bīt-Zamāni. I besieged the city. My warriors flew like bird(s) against them. I felled 600 of their combat troops with the sword and cut off their heads. I captured 400 of their soldiers alive. I brought out 3,000 captives from them. I took that city in hand for myself. I took the live soldiers and the heads to the city Amedu, his royal city, and built a pile of heads before his gate. I impaled the live soldiers on stakes around about his city. 1 fought my way inside his gate and cut down his orchards.

Moving on from the city Amedu I entered the pass of Mount Kasiiari at the city Allabsia wherein none of the kings my fathers had ever set foot, I approached the city Udu, the fortified city of Labturu, son of Tupusu. I besieged the city and conquered it by means of tunnels, siege-towers, and battering rams. I felled with the sword 1,400 of their fighting men. I captured 780 soldiers alive. I brought out 3,000 captives from them. I impaled the live soldiers on stakes around about his city. 1 gouged out the eyes of some and the remainder I uprooted and brought to Assyria.

III THE GOD MANIFEST BECOMES IMMORTAL

INCANTATION TO NINURTA, DAGAN AND UTULU

To the god Ninurta, the strong, the almighty, the exalted, foremost among the gods, the splendid and perfect warrior whose attack in battle is unequalled, the eldest son who commands battle (skills), offspring of the god Nudimmud, warrior of the Igigu gods, the capable, prince of the gods, offspring of Ekur, the one who holds the bond of heaven and underworld, the one who opens springs, the one who walks the wide underworld, the god without whom no decisions are taken in heaven and underworld, the swift, the ferocious, the one whose command is unalterable, foremost in the (four) quarters, the one who gives scepter and (powers of) decision to all cities, the stern canal-inspector whose utterance cannot be altered, extensively capable, sage of the gods, the noble, the god Utulu, lord of lords, into whose hands is entrusted the circumference of heaven and underworld, king of battle, the hero who rejoices in battles, the triumphant, the perfect, lord of springs and seas, the angry and merciless whose attack is a deluge, the one who overwhelms enemy lands and fells the wicked, the splendid god who never changes (his mind), light of heaven and underworld who illuminates the interior of the *apsû*, annihilator of the evil, subduer of the insubmissive, destroyer of enemies, the one whose command none of the gods in the divine assembly can alter, bestower of life, the compassionate god to whom it is good to pray, the one who dwells in the city Calah, great lord, my lord: Ashurnasirpal, king of the universe, unrivalled king, king of all the four quarters, sun(god) of all people, chosen of the gods Enlil and Ninurta, beloved of the gods Anu and Dagan, destructive weapon of the great gods, the pious, beloved of (20) your (Ninurta's) heart, prince, favorite of the god Enlil, whose priesthood is pleasing to your great divinity and whose reign you established, valiant man who acts with the support of Aššur, his lord, and has no rival among the princes of the four quarters, marvelous shepherd, fearless in battle, mighty flood-tide which has no opponent, the king who subdues those insubordinate to him, who rules all peoples, strong male, who treads upon the necks of his foes, trampler of all enemies, the one who breaks up the forces of the rebellious, he who acts with the support of the great gods, his lords, and has conquered all lands, gained dominion over the highlands in their entirety and received their tribute, capturer of hostages, he who is victorious over all lands.

When Aššur, the lord who called my name and who makes my sovereignty supreme, placed his merciless weapon in my lordly arms I felled with the sword the extensive troops of the Lullumu in battle. With the help of the gods Šamaš and Adad, the gods my supporters, I thundered like the god Adad, the devastator, against the troops of the lands Nairi, Habhu, the Subaru, and the land Nirbu, The king who subdued (the territory stretching) from the opposite bank of the Tigris to Mount Lebanon and the Great Sea, the entire land Laqû, and the land Suhu including the city Rapiqu: he conquered from the source of the River Subnat to the source of the Tigris. I brought within the boundaries of my land (the territory stretching) from the passes of Mount Kirruru to the land Gilzānu, from the opposite bank of the Lower Zab to the city Tīl-Bāri which is upstream from the city Zaban, from the city Tīl-ša-Abtāni to the city Trl-ša-Zabdāni, the cities Hirimu, Harutu, (which are) fortresses of Karduniaš. I accounted (the people) from the passes of Mount Babitu to Mount ('the city') Hašmar as people of my land. In the lands over which I gained dominion I always appointed my governors. They entered (lit, 'performed') servitude and I imposed upon them corvée.

Aššur, the great lord, king of all the great gods; god Anu, foremost in strength, the one who decrees destinies; god Ea, king of the *apsû*, lord of wisdom and understanding; god Sîn, wise one, lord of the lunar disk, lofty luminary; god Marduk, sage, lord god of oracles; god Adad, strong, almighty among the gods, exalted; god Ninurta, hero, warrior of the gods, the one who lays low the wicked; god Nusku, bearer of the holy scepter, circumspect god; goddess Ninlil, spouse of the god Enlil, mother of the great gods; god Nergal, perfect one, king of battle; god Enlil, exalted one, father of the gods, creator of all; god Šamaš, judge of heaven and underworld, commander of all; (i 10) goddess Ištar, foremost in heaven and underworld, who is consummate in the canons of combat; (I, Ashurnasirpal), attentive prince, worshipper of the great gods, ferocious dragon, conqueror of cities and the entire highlands, king of lords, controller of the obstinate, crowned with splendour, fearless in battle, lofty and merciless hero, he who stirs up strife, king of all princes, lord of lords, chief herdsman, king of kings, attentive purification priest, designate of the warrior god Ninurta, destructive weapon of the great gods, avenger, the king who has always acted justly with the support of Aššur and the god Šamaš, the gods who help him, and cut down like marsh reeds fortified mountains and princes hostile to him and subdued all their lands, provider of offerings for the great gods, legitimate prince, to whom is perpetually entrusted the proper administration of the rites of the temples of his land, whose deeds and offerings the great gods of heaven and underworld love so that they (therefore) established forever his priesthood in the temples, granted to his dominion their fierce weapons, and made him more marvelous than (any of) the kings of the four quarters with respect to the splendor of his weapons and the radiance of his dominion, (he who) has always contested with all enemies of Aššur above and below and imposed upon them tribute and tax, conqueror of the foes of Aššur, strong king, king of Assyria; son of Tukultl-Ninurta (II), vice-regent of Aššur, who defeated all his enemies and hung the corpses of his enemies on posts, grandson of Adad-nārāri (II), appointee of the great gods, who always achieved the defeat of those insubmissive to him and (thereby) became lord of all, offspring of Aššur-dān (II) who opened towns and founded shrines: him, I, the king, capable in battle, vanquisher of cities and (i 40) highlands, foremost in battle, king of the four quarters, the one who defeats his enemies, the one who disintegrates all his enemies, king of the totality of the (four) quarters including all their princes, the king who forces to bow down those insubmissive to him, the one who rules all peoples; these destinies came forth at the command of the great gods and they properly fixed (them) as my destinies. Because of my voluntary offerings and my prayers the goddess Istar, the mistress who loves my priesthood, approved of me and she made up her mind to make war and battle, bestowed the tablets of destiny to me and of which I drank deep of her blood.

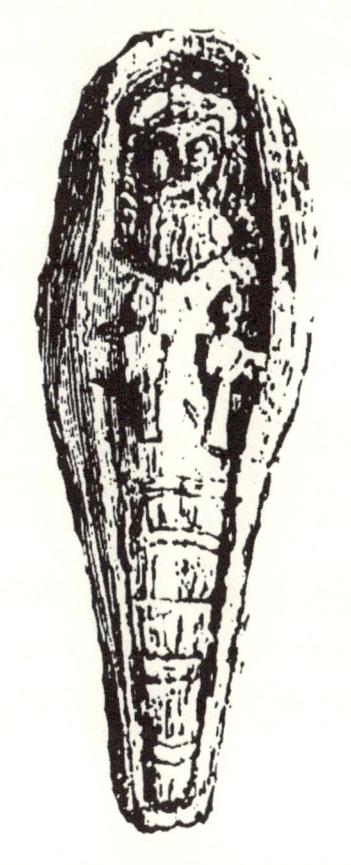

IV THE DARKNESS

This being the record of the Priests of Tiamat the Hidden, the cult of Ishtar of Arbela. It is our record to present the majesty of our great Mother. Ashurnasirpal, the Great King, the Musmah has become truly the Son of Tiamat and entered the great darkness. Ashurnasirpal shall dwell in the Great City of Irkalla, our great temple shall give unto him the blood which shall quench his great thirst. The land of dreams shall adorn him in glory, for his rising will be again in the flesh of another King. For the great offerings to the gods will forever keep the powers of both darkness and light in great splendor in all of our days and beyond. For if the temples are destroyed and the gods offended, we shall still be as the mighty storm which cannot be calmed or sated. The underworld and mountains beyond will be our resting place, in your flesh we shall live yet again!

THE GATE IS OPEN

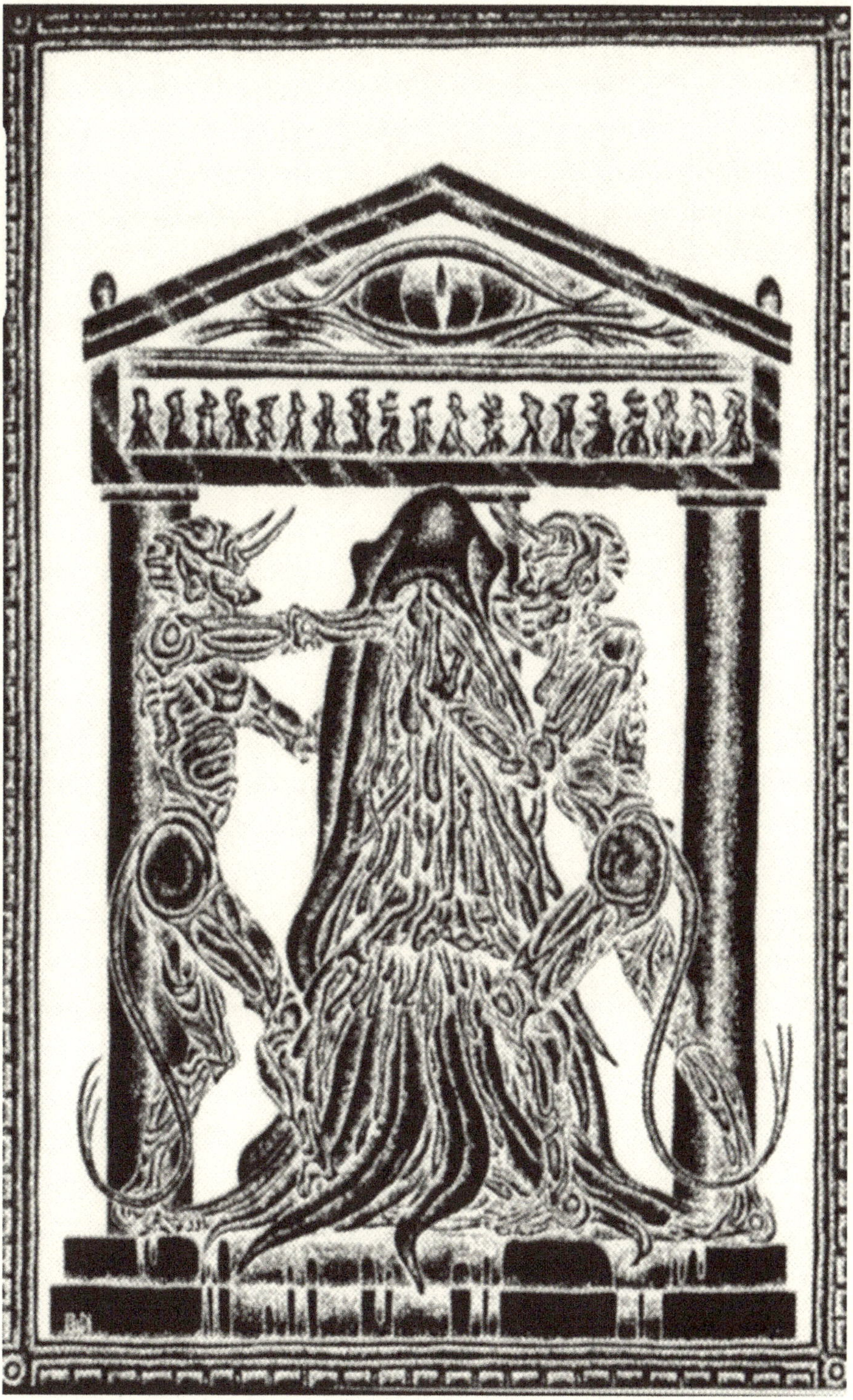

ABOUT THE AUTHOR

Mr. Ford is most known for his occult books which have been translated in three different languages! Michael W. Ford is the author of Maskim Hul – Babylonian Magick, Adversarial Light-Magick of the Nephilim, The Bible of the Adversary, Liber HVHI, Gates of Dozak, Luciferian Witchcraft and many more titles. Mr. Ford has a taste for all things horror, macabre and of course the occult.

THANK YOU:

Hope Marie, Artists Nestor Avalos, Kristian Wahlin, Karl N.E. (I am sorry to all three of you for the delay in publication), Stephen Sennitt, Tomas Tabori for his valuable editing assistance, my fans and friends worldwide.

For those Not Afraid of the Dark...

www.luciferianwitchcraft.com